THE COMPLETE CLASSIC ADVENTURES BY ALEX TOTH
VOLUME ONE

That night Zorro rides hard for the pueblo, realizing the danger to everyone in Los Angeles...

ZORRO
Volume One of the
Classic Adventures
by Alex Toth

Authorized edition adapted from
the Walt Disney television series
based on the famous character
created by Johnston McCulley

Published by:
Little Eva Ink
217 E. 85th St. Suite 101
New York, NY 10028

First printing July 1998 by Image Comics

ISBN# 1-58240-014-8

Edited by Dean Mullaney and Renee Witterstaetter
Design and color by Peter Poplaski
Production and gray tints by Raymond Fehrenbach
from guides produced by Alex Toth

The Classic Alex Toth Zorro, volume 1, number 1, July 1998.
Published by Little Eva Ink for Image Comics, 217 East 85th
St. Suite 101, New York, NY 10028. Zorro copyright© and
trademark Zorro Productions. All rights reserved. The story,
characters and incidents mentioned in this magazine are
entirely fictional. With the excetion of artwork used for review
purposes, none of the contents of this publication may be
reprinted without the permission of Zorro Productions and
Image Comics. Publisher and creators assume no responsibility
for unsolicited materials. Printed in Canada.

CONTENTS

Introduction by Howard Chaykin
page 7

Presenting Señor Zorro
page 11

Zorro's Secret Passage
page 29

The Ghost of the Mission, part one
page 43

The Ghost of the Mission, part two
page 56

Garcia's Secret
page 69

The King's Emissary
page 83

A Bad Day for Bernardo
page 95

The Little Zorro
page 101

The Visitor
page 107

A Double for Diego
page 113

Introduction

I'm sure "Zorro" conjures up a lot of different things to different people —from the old Street & Smith pulp covers, to Douglas Fairbanks (Senior, not Junior, of course, and how *did* he do all those great stunts with such tiny feet?) leaping all the hell over the place, to Tyrone Power doing his level best to be Errol Flynn. I'll bet there's even some chucklehead out there who thinks "Zorro, the Gay Blade" was a funny movie! (If so, and you're reading this —out. Now.) For me, "Zorro" means two things —the single best episode of the old "Bob Newhart" show, and the wonderful adaptations of the Disney television series by Alex Toth.

If we accept as fact the old dictum/gag, "What's the Golden Age of Science Fiction? Why, twelve, of course!" and apply it to comics (and certainly on the basis of the number of thirtysomething-ish/rapidly aging superhero comic book fan geeks running around, still obsessed with the same semi-literate junk they read when they were twelve, one must accept this as fact) then I must cop to at least some guilt in this particular department.

When I was twelve, my fellow fanboy geeks and I had our favorites, and, unfortunately for the revisionists, Jack Kirby, Frank Frazetta, and Will Eisner weren't among them. How could they be—we never heard of any of those guys. The four best artists (even then, comics fans didn't know the difference between "favorite" and "best") were Gil Kane, Carmine Infantino, Joe Kubert, and last, and certainly best, Alex Toth.

Now, unlike those other guys, Toth didn't do any of the regular superhero strips like **Green Lantern, Flash,** or **Hawkman.** If memory serves me correctly, the first Toth feature I ever saw was "Eclipso"—one of the strangest looking superhero strips I'd ever seen—possibly because of Alex's geographic location in Southern California, giving the feature an unusual non-urban quality. At any rate, it was odd looking—chunky, rich blacks, bold textures, and a contour line as vigorous as a butcher's swing at a chopping block. (Mind you,

these are an allegedly mature adult's observations —back then, we just thought it was hot stuff.) And for those beginning days of puberty, this guy Toth did some of the cutest girls in comics.

Which, considering the number of more than attractive damsels in distress, brings us back to **Zorro**.

Dell Comics were never very widely distributed in my neighborhood in Brooklyn (maybe because, as the tag line went, "Dell comics are good comics"—mmm boy, they had slogans then) so, even though I was a big fan of the Disney **Zorro** show (Thursday night at seven-thirty, ABC-TV, brought to you by Seven-Up, with this really weird animated bird character named Freshup Freddy—like I say, they had slogans then), I never saw these stories on their first go-round. By the time I'd become aware of the existence of a **Zorro** comic book, we'd already outgrown such infantile stuff and gone on to those notoriously grown up Marvel comics—and furthermore, Dell (now Western) used photos of Guy Williams in his Zorro suit on the covers, so I had no idea of the interior contents. So, one summer, spending the weekend at my Grandmother's place on Staten Island (or "The Country" as we Brooklynites called it), bored out of my mind waiting for the next all action ish of Stan & Jack's **Fantastic Four**, I pulled one of these **Zorro** books off the rack, opened it to the splash and, suffice to say, my brains fell out.

What I had there was prime Alex Toth—so this is what he'd been doing while all those other guys were drawing all that other stuff for DC. Who knew? I went berserk—and started a Toth acquisition binge which continues to this day.

At any rate, Toth's **Zorro** is Alex at his very best—particularly considering the rather restrictive sensibilities imposed on talent by Dell Comics. As always, his draughtmanship is extraordinary—by this I don't mean that masturbatory rendering so beloved by too many comics fans, who seem to judge the quality of work by the number of lines— but instead, a gift of staging, of the placement of figures and objects in space, combined with an uncanny strength of characterization, making Alex an object of acute envy for any artist with half a brain.

In addition to and in support of these considerable abilities, however, is an obvious love of the source material. Although Alex is certainly the most modern of comics artists—an illustrator in the truest sense, with a line usually most at home with contemporary subjects—his love of swashbuckling films and themes comes through loud and clear in these pieces.

Anyone who has any familiarity with his body of work knows of Alex's lifelong obsession with Errol Flynn (take a peek at his "Bravo for Adventure" stories, for instance)—and anyone who has met the man himself knows that, under that carefully crafted curmudgeonly exterior, beats the heart of a self-styled Romantic Cavalier—always on his best behaviour in the company of the ladies (sorry, in this case not women, but ladies)—and always ready to drop the chivalry like a hot potato as soon as the ladies are out of earshot.

So, to a great extent, this work stands as a contradictory watershed in a brilliant career—an acutely sharp-edged modernist, deeply influenced by industrial design, producing work overtly tinged with the chivalric attitudes of those swashbuckling epics of his youth. But, knowing Alex as I do, perhaps it's not quite so contradictory after all . . . and maybe that Golden Age of Science Fiction (or Comics, in this case) applies to Alex, too.

In closing, when Dean Mullaney, publisher of these reprints, asked me to write this introduction, I was delighted, to say the very least —and flattered as all get out. One rarely gets an assignment in the comics business as easy as saying nice things about Alex Toth's work is for me —when, suddenly, I started a month long, sustained moment of panic. Why, you ask . . .?

Simply put, I realized that anything I said about Alex—and I do mean anything, positive or negative—might very well tick him off. He is, contrary to those of you out there who think I hold the title, the single most opinionated, cantankerous and hardheaded guy in comics. So I thought long and hard about it, finally deciding to throw caution to the winds, and dove in headfirst.

I thought back to my first meeting with his Nibs, back in August of 1975. We were introduced by a mutual friend, David Armstrong (Hi, Dave! Rita! How're the ki—oops, I digress!) who brought me to Alex's Hollywood home late one afternoon after the San Diego convention. I was all prepared for Alex's attitude—I'd read that great interview in **Graphic Story Magazine**—and I was committed to not being cowed by this guy, no matter who he thought he was.

Forget it.

He had me on the ropes and on the run from word one and, before I knew it, he had me defending the work of guys I loathed. Why? How? I couldn't begin to tell you. At any rate, the afternoon passed quickly—and argumentatively— as I, noted big mouth Young Turk, gave ground on every single point. I couldn't for the life of me tell you exactly what it is we argued about (Alex probably could, being that kind of guy) but finally, it came time to tip out . . . at which point he pulled out a sheaf of original pages from "The Land Unknown," a truly wonderful art job adapting a truly awful Jock Mahoney dinosaur movie—and told me to pick one. I nearly shit a whale—a Toth original!!!

I picked a favorite from the pile, which Alex took from me to autograph. He handed me the signed original and I left with Dave, not bothering to look at the inscription as I shook Alex's hand at the door.

As we drove away, I took another look at my page—a stunning piece of artwork, which, along with my Cornwall, Fawcett, and Beckhoff, is among my most prized possessions—and read the inscription. It read, "Howie (yes, *Howie*—Alex can get away with that), you're still wrong—Alex."

True to form, the bandit had gotten the last word.

Somewhere in Los Angeles,

Howard Victor Chaykin

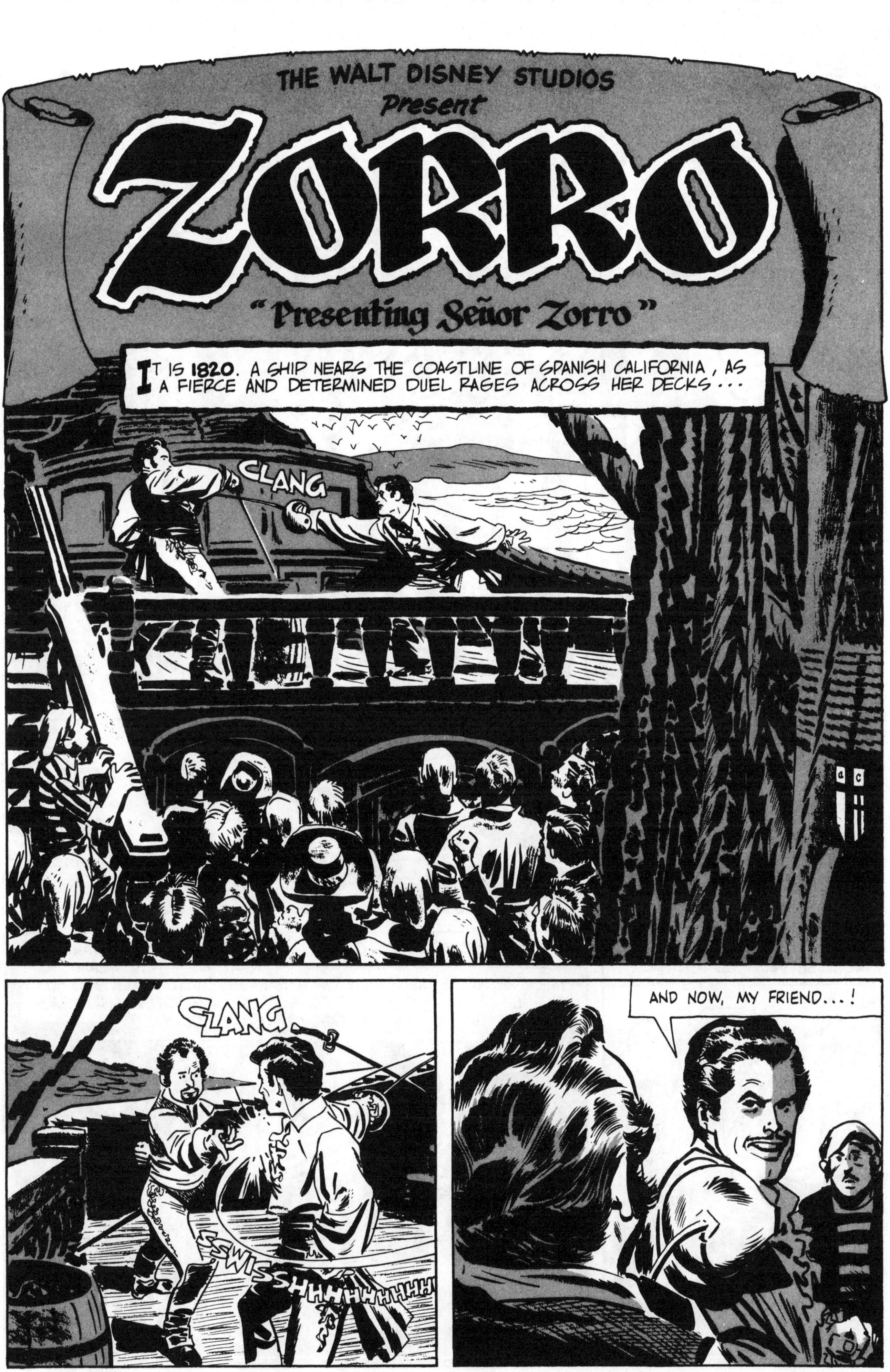

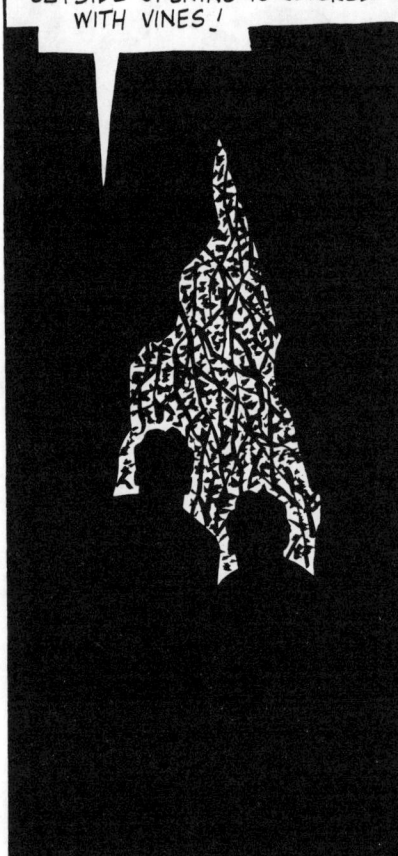

"VERY CONVENIENT, MY YOUNG FRIEND! DID ANYBODY SEE YOU ON THIS TRIP TO THE HILLS?" "I-I WENT ALONE!"	"YOU LIE, BENITO! YOU ARE THE OUTLAW, ZORRO! ADMIT IT!" "NO! NO! BENITO IS NOT AN OUTLAW! I SAW HIM LAST NIGHT! HE WAS WALKING WITH SEÑORITA TORRES!"
"BE QUIET, PEPITO!... THE BOY IS MAKING THIS UP, SEÑOR!" "THIS IS VERY INTERESTING! PERHAPS WE SHOULD GO TO SEÑORITA TORRES... AND TEST THIS UNTRUTH!"	"TAKE HIM OUT... TO THE TORRES RANCHO!" "GO WITH THEM, BENITO! I KNOW YOU ARE INNOCENT! WE SHALL PROVE IT!"
IT IS DARK AS MONASTARIO'S MEN, WITH BENITO, REACH CASA DE TORRES... "GOOD EVENING, SEÑORITA! WE HAVE BUSINESS WITH YOU!" "OH! BENITO! WHAT IS WRONG?"	"I'LL TELL YOU! WE BELIEVE BENITO IS THE BANDIT ZORRO! BUT WE HEARD THAT BENITO WAS WITH YOU LAST NIGHT! PERHAPS YOU WOULD TELL US THE TRUTH!" "I'VE TOLD YOU! I SCARCELY KNOW THE SEÑORITA!"

Panel 1	Panel 2	Panel 3

Panel 1: IN *THAT* CASE, WE MAY ASSUME THAT YOU *ARE* ZORRO AND *WERE* IN THE PUEBLO *LAST NIGHT*!

NO... *NO*! BENITO IS *NOT* A BANDIT! HE *WAS* WITH ME LAST NIGHT! I SWEAR IT!

Panel 2: *ENOUGH* OF THIS! I WILL TRY ONCE MORE TO PROVE WE HAVE THE RIGHT MAN! GARCIA, STATION YOUR MEN ABOUT THE HOUSE! IF HE IS ZORRO I CAN TELL BY HIS *SWORDSMANSHIP*!

YES, COMMANDANTE!

Panel 3: AT THAT MINUTE, RIDING HIS GREAT BLACK STALLION ACROSS THE PLAINS... ZORRO!

Panel 4: WHO MINUTES LATER, IS OVERLOOKING THE TORRES RANCHO...

I HEAR SWORDPLAY INSIDE THE HOUSE... AND THERE IS SERGEANT GARCIA! I'LL HAVE TO REMOVE HIM TEMPORARILY!

Panel 5: I WONDER... I DON'T SUPPOSE HE'D WANT TO LOSE HIS HORSE AND HAVE TO WALK BACK TO THE CUARTEL... BUT...

Panel 6: WAP WHINNEEE

WAIT! COME BACK!
NOW TO SEE WHAT THE WILY COMMANDANTE IS UP TO!
YOU PUT UP A GOOD FIGHT, VAQUERO! BUT YOU'RE NO MATCH FOR ME!
STOP! STOP! YOU'VE HURT BENITO!
UH...!
AHA! THE GREAT ZORRO IS DOWN!
NO, COMMANDANTE! BENITO IS DOWN, NOT ZORRO! YOU'VE BEEN LOOKING FOR ME?
WHAT...?
SWISH
CLANG
GARCIA! GET YOUR MEN! IT IS ZORRO!
CLANG

GARCIA! GARCIA!
WHAT'S THIS? SOUNDS LIKE THE COMMANDANTE IS IN TROUBLE!
THIS BENITO... HE IS A GOOD SWORDSMAN, MI CAPITAN?
YOU IDIOT! THIS ISN'T BENITO! IT IS THE REAL ZORRO! SHOOT HIM! SHOOT!
THE... THE REAL ZORRO?...YES, S-SIR...I'LL...I'LL... SH-SHOOT...!
SWISH
CLANG
STOP! STOP!
BAM
BLAM
TORNADO! HERE!
WHINNEEEEE
BAM
BLAM
GET THE MEN! STOP HIM!

YI-I-I-I-I!	TO HORSE YOU **FOOLS!** AFTER HIM!	I DON'T WANT TO LEAD THEM TO MY SECRET PASSAGE! HMM! THERE **IS ANOTHER** WAY...!

YOU'VE **GOT** TO MAKE IT ACROSS THIS CHASM, BOY! IT'S THE **ONLY** WAY WE'LL **LOSE** THEM!

THAT'S IT, TORNADO! **UP** AND **OVER!**

HE MOCKS US ON THE OTHER SIDE!... **JUMP**, MEN! **JUMP!** IF **HE** CAN MAKE IT, WHY CAN'T **YOU?**

I-I'M SORRY, MI 'CAPITAN, BUT MY HORSE WILL NOT JUMP THIS CHASM!
COWARDS! SPREAD OUT, THEN! WE'LL CUT HIM OFF!
HOURS LATER, MONASTARIO'S WEARY PARTY STOPS AT CASA DE LA VEGA...
SEÑOR DE LA VEGA! HOLA!
WHAT? WHY ARE YOU HERE, COMMANDANTE?
WE SEARCH FOR THE OUTLAW, ZORRO! HE'S IN THIS AREA!!
BUT I THOUGHT YOU HAD HIM... OUR CAPORAL, BENITO! DID HE ESCAPE?
NO! BENITO IS NOT ZORRO!! WELL, GOOD NIGHT, SEÑOR!
IT'S ALL YOUR FAULT, SERGEANT! YOU SHOULD HAVE KNOWN BENITO WAS NOT ZORRO!
YES, COMMANDANTE...!!

WALT DISNEY PRESENTS ZORRO

The Ghost of the Mission.. part One

THE LITTLE PUEBLO OF LOS ANGELES APPEARS PEACEFUL, BUT INSIDE THE WALLED CUARTEL, THE LAW SEETHES ANGRILY... VOWING ITS REVENGE ON THE ELUSIVE *ZORRO*, WHO HAS SNATCHED THE FALSELY-ACCUSED CAPTIVE, DON NACHO TORRES, FROM UNDER ITS VERY NOSE! THEN, SUDDENLY...

LET ME IN! LET ME IN! I MUST SEE THE COMANDANTE! I HAVE NEWS OF TORRES!

STOP! YOU CANNOT ENTER UNLESS...!

WHAT'S THIS? YOU KNOW WHERE TORRES IS HIDING?

YES! YES! HE IS AT THE MISSION OF SAN GABRIEL! I SAW HIM THERE MYSELF, ONLY THIS MORNING!

I HAVE HEARD THERE IS A REWARD FOR WORD OF TORRES! I WANT IT, COMANDANTE MONASTARIO!

HERE IS YOUR REWARD! NOW GET OUT OF THE WAY! WE'RE RIDING TO THE MISSION AT ONCE!

A SHORT TIME LATER, DON DIEGO DE LA VEGA AND HIS VALET, BERNARDO, ARE RIDING TO LOS ANGELES...

YES! I SEE, BERNARDO! IT LOOKS LIKE CAPITAN MONASTARIO'S LANCERS!

THE LANCERS CHARGE BY, FORCING DIEGO'S CARRIAGE OFF THE ROAD...

THEY'RE HEADING FOR THE MISSION, BERNARDO! I DON'T LIKE THE LOOKS OF THIS! WE MUST GO BACK! QUICKLY!	MEANWHILE, AT THE MISSION... **BONNNNNNNG** THE CHURCH BELL! BUT...IT'S MUCH TOO EARLY FOR THE ANGELUS!...
IT WAS THE WARNING BELL, PADRE FELIPE! LOOK! MONASTARIO'S LANCERS! / QUICKLY, SEÑOR TORRES! INTO THE CHURCH! THEY MUSTN'T SEE YOU!	SURROUND THE AREA, MEN! SERGEANT GARCIA, I WILL HOLD YOU PERSONALLY RESPONSIBLE IF TORRES GETS AWAY! / ER...YES, MI CAPITAN!
BUENOS DIAS, CAPITAN! DID YOU BRING YOUR MEN TO WHITEWASH THE CHURCH? IT TRULY NEEDS...!	WE HAVE COME TO ARREST DON NACHO TORRES, IN THE NAME OF THE CROWN! / ARREST HIM?... THEN I AM HERE TO PROTECT HIS SANCTUARY, IN THE NAME OF THE CROSS!

AHA! THEN YOU ADMIT HE IS HERE! BUT THIS SANCTUARY LAW IS SO ABSURD!
NOT TO SEÑOR TORRES! DURING HIS PERIOD OF SANCTUARY, YOU MAY NOT MOLEST HIM!
BAH! WHO WOULD KNOW IF I TOOK HIM BY FORCE? WE'RE A LONG WAYS FROM MADRID OR ROME!
BUT YOU WOULD NEVER GET AWAY WITH IT! YOU KNOW THAT, COMANDANTE!
MAYBE! MAYBE NOT! BUT I WILL LEAVE HIM FOR NOW! YOU CANNOT GIVE HIM SANCTUARY FOREVER, PADRE!
ONLY FOR FORTY DAYS, CAPITAN! I HOPE THAT WILL BE LONG ENOUGH TO PROVE HE IS INNOCENT!
DIEGO AND BERNARDO SOON ARRIVE AT THE MISSION...
WHAT GOES ON HERE, CAPITAN? IS THE ARMY ON MANEUVERS?
WHY ARE YOU HERE, DIEGO?
WHY, I HEARD THAT PADRE FELIPE HAS SOME ORANGES TO SELL! I AM HERE TO BUY SOME!
OH? PERHAPS IT MIGHT INTEREST YOU TO KNOW THAT SEÑOR TORRES HAS TAKEN SANCTUARY IN THE CHURCH!
I SEE! BUT THAT DOESN'T INTEREST ME! I AM LOOKING FOR ORANGES!
THAT IS GOOD! IT IS BETTER THAT YOUNG MEN LIKE YOU MIND THEIR OWN BUSINESS!

MINUTES LATER... DIEGO! I AM GLAD TO SEE YOU! IS THE ARMY STILL OUTSIDE?

IN FULL FORCE! BUT I WANTED TO TELL YOU, I'VE CALLED ON YOUR FAMILY, REASSURING THEM OF YOUR SAFETY, TORRES!

THANK YOU, MY FRIEND! BUT IT SEEMS HOPELESS! ALL I DID WAS SPEAK OUT AGAINST CORRUPTION! AND NOW I'M ACCUSED OF **TREASON**!

BUT WE ALL KNOW YOU ARE **NOT** GUILTY OF TREASON, DON NACHO! IF ONLY THERE WERE SOME WAY TO HELP YOU...! SO FAR, ONLY THIS SHOW-OFF, ZORRO, HAS...

HA! WITHOUT ZORRO, I PROBABLY WOULD NOT BE ALIVE TODAY! TAKE MY ADVICE, DIEGO! STAY WITH YOUR BOOKS AND GUITARS! OR YOU, TOO, WILL END UP LIKE THIS!

EEYAAAAAHHHHHH!

WHAT'S THAT?

DROP THOSE ORANGES AND MOVE ALONG THERE!

ONTO THE ROAD! MOVE! FAST!

STOP! YOU'VE NO RIGHT TO DO THIS!

IT'S NO USE, PADRE! I'M TAKING EVERY INDIAN I CAN FIND!
BUT THEY ARE LIKE CHILDREN! THEY LIVE AND WORK AT THE MISSION! YOU CAN'T DO THIS, I TELL YOU!
OH, NO? THERE IS AN ORDER OF THE KING THAT STATES A COMANDANTE MAY DRAFT ALL AVAILABLE LABOR WHENEVER HE CONSIDERS IT NECESSARY!
DON'T TAKE OUT YOUR WRATH ON THESE POOR, SIMPLE PEOPLE! I BEG YOU, CAPTAIN! ALL THEY KNOW IS TO PICK ORANGES AND...!
BAH! THE ORANGES ARE SOUR, ANYWAY!
LINE THEM UP OVER THERE! AND HAND OUT THE TOOLS!
THE DETAIL IS READY FOR WORK, CAPITAN!
GOOD! I WANT A NEW ROAD BUILT, GARCIA!
A ROAD, CAPITAN? WHERE?
HAVE THEM START RIGHT HERE... THROUGH THERE... TO THE OTHER SIDE OF THERE!

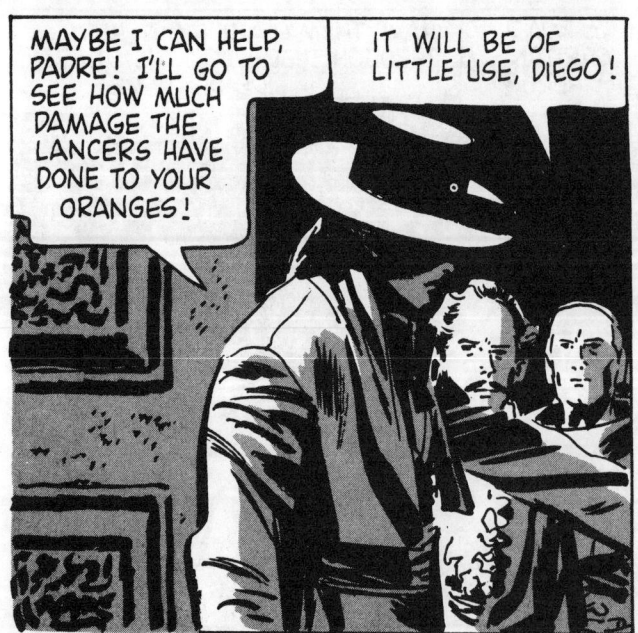

THERE... THROUGH TO THERE? BUT THE OLD ROAD GOES VERY NICELY TO THE SAME PLACE, MI CAPITÁN! OVER *HERE*! THAT'S RIGHT! BUT WE WILL BUILD *ANOTHER* ONE!	ALL THOSE ROCKS ARE IN THE WAY OF ANOTHER ROAD, SIR! THAT'S WHY WE NEED THE INDIANS TO MOVE THE ROCKS, YOU IDIOT! NOW GET THEM TO WORK!
PADRE FELIPE! THERE WILL BE MORE TROUBLE THAN I AM WORTH! I MUST GIVE MYSELF UP!	NO, DON NACHO! YOU MUST STAY HERE, INSIDE! AT LEAST, WAIT UNTIL NIGHTFALL! PERHAPS THE PADRE AND I WILL THINK OF SOME PLAN! YES, DIEGO IS RIGHT! YOU MUST STAY! WE WILL THINK OF SOMETHING!
MAYBE I CAN HELP, PADRE! I'LL GO TO SEE HOW MUCH DAMAGE THE LANCERS HAVE DONE TO YOUR ORANGES! IT WILL BE OF LITTLE USE, DIEGO!	PRESENTLY... AH! THERE IS BERNARDO! AND HE IS LOOKING THIS WAY!

BERNARDO! WE MUST WORK FAST! GET BACK TO THE CAVE! BRING ME TORNADO AS QUICKLY AS YOU CAN! I DON'T KNOW WHAT ZORRO WILL ACCOMPLISH TONIGHT... BUT SOMETHING MUST BE DONE!
THAT NIGHT, AS THE INDIANS ARE FORCED TO CONTINUE WORKING...
HERE! THIS WILL GIVE YOU STRENGTH!
I AM SORRY, PADRE! BUT THE COMANDANTE HAS GIVEN THE ORDERS!
AND NEAR THE MISSION ORANGE GROVE...
AH, IT IS FULLY DARK! BERNARDO SHOULD BE BACK WITH TORNADO... AND HIDING OUTSIDE!
DIEGO! WHAT ARE YOU DOING HERE AT THIS TIME OF NIGHT?
WHAT? OH, I- ER- I ONLY THOUGHT I SHOULD HELP PADRE FELIPE WITH HIS WORK, CAPITAN!
HA! YOU'RE A VIRTUOUS YOUNG MAN! BUT THIS IS UNCALLED FOR!
THESE ORANGES WILL FREEZE! YOU'VE TAKEN AWAY ALL OF THE PADRE'S HELPERS!
THAT IS JUST THE BEGINNING, DIEGO! IF WE HAVE TO, WE'LL WORK THOSE INDIANS UNTIL THEY DROP... UNLESS YOU CAN CONVINCE TORRES TO GIVE HIMSELF UP!
PERHAPS I CAN DO THAT, CAPITAN!

GOOD! THAT IS THE ONLY WAY YOU CAN HELP PADRE FELIPE, DIEGO!	BERNARDO! YOU HAVE BROUGHT TORNADO? ON THE OTHER SIDE OF THE WALL? GOOD! THERE'S MUCH TO BE DONE! LISTEN, HERE'S WHAT WE'LL DO...!

MEANWHILE... GOOD WORK! MOST OF THE ROCKS HAVE BEEN MOVED TO THE OTHER SIDE! NOW HAVE THE INDIANS MOVE THEM BACK AGAIN!

WHAT? BACK AGAIN? BUT WHY, CAPITAN?

JUST DO AS I SAY, IDIOT!... I WILL PERSONALLY ASK TORRES IF HE IS READY TO GIVE HIMSELF UP!

MINUTES LATER... SEÑOR TORRES! I HAVE NOT COME TO HARM YOU! ONLY TO SEE IF DON DIEGO HAS TOLD YOU OF...!

AT THAT MOMENT, THE LOUD RESONANT TONES OF THE CHURCH ORGAN BREAK FORTH IN MELODY...

WHAT...?

SHHHHHHH! DO NOT DISTURB DON NACHO NOW, MONASTARIO!
THEN YOU HAVEN'T SPOKEN TO HIM?
VRROOMMMMM
OH, YES! AND IT LOOKS LIKE YOU'VE WON! SO AS THIS IS HIS LAST VISIT TO THE CHURCH, PERHAPS YOU WILL WAIT, UNTIL HE IS READY TO GO!
OF COURSE! I DON'T MIND WAITING A BIT LONGER AS LONG AS HE IS GIVING HIMSELF UP!
DON NACHO WANTED TO HEAR MY MUSIC ONCE MORE! HE'S ALWAYS LOVED BACH! WHAT ABOUT YOU, CAPITAN?
NEVER MIND THAT! JUST FINISH PLAYING AS SOON AS YOU CAN!
OUTSIDE...
STOP MAKING NOISES WITH THAT WHIP! LISTEN TO THE ORGAN MUSIC! IS IT NOT BEAUTIFUL?
WHILE GARCIA AND HIS SOLDIERS STAND ENTHRALLED BY THE MAJESTIC TONES OF THE ORGAN...
SHHH! PUT DOWN THE ROCK! RUN INTO THE HILLS! QUIETLY!
AH! NOW IF ONLY DIEGO CAN PLAY LONG ENOUGH...!

WHAT IS THIS? *STOP! STOP! I SAY STOP!*	NO! DO NOT SHOOT! **BLAM!!**
WHAT... WHAT HAPPENED? HOW MANY GOT AWAY? WATCH THE OTHERS! GET THEM ALL TOGETHER! HURRY UP!	SERGEANT GARCIA! WHO FIRED THAT SHOT? *GARCIA! ANSWER ME!*
TWO INDIANS ESCAPED, CAPITAN! BUT IT WAS NOT MY FAULT! I... / NEVER MIND! GET THE OTHERS BACK TO WORK!	YOU! COME WITH ME! WE'LL BRING THOSE INDIANS BACK BY THEIR THUMBS! / YES, MI CAPITAN!

IN THE CONFUSION, PADRE FELIPE HAS RUN BACK TO THE MISSION AND TORRES...

THIS IS TOO MUCH, PADRE! I MUST GIVE MYSELF UP TO PREVENT MORE TROUBLE!

NO, NO, TORRES! YOU MUST NOT!

SENTRY! CALL YOUR CAPITAN BACK! STOP ALL THIS! I AM YOUR PRISONER!

WHAT?

SERGEANT GARCIA! COME QUICKLY! I HAVE TORRES!

I'LL STAND BY YOU, DON NACHO, AS LONG AS I CAN! YOU ARE A BRAVE MAN!

WHAT?...YOU HAVE TORRES? AT LAST! I WILL RIDE TO TELL THE CAPITAN! HE...!

SUDDENLY, A BLACK RIDER CHARGES PAST...

UH...WH-WHAT'S THAT...??

IT'S... ZORRO!

RUN! RUN! ALL OF YOU! FOR THE HILLS!

IT IS ZORRO!

DO AS HE SAYS! RUN!

WE ARE SAVED!

ZORRO'S WHIP SNAPS OUT...
BLAM
CRACK!
YIIIIIII!
AFTER THEM, MEN! TO YOUR HORSES! GET YOUR HORSES!
AH! BERNARDO DID A GOOD JOB OF CUTTING THEIR REINS!
COME BACK, HORSES! STOP!
CRACK!!
BACK INSIDE THE MISSION, TORRES! THE INDIANS HAVE ESCAPED! THERE'S NO REASON FOR YOU TO GIVE YOURSELF UP!
YOU MAY FRIGHTEN MY SOLDIERS, SEÑOR ZORRO, BUT YOU WON'T FIND ME SO EASY TO HANDLE!
THAT REMAINS TO BE SEEN, CAPITAN!
WH-WHAT...?

UFFFFFF!! H-HELP! HA HA HAHAHA HA HA	**THERE'S NO ONE TO HELP YOU, CAPITAN! MAY YOU HAVE A SPEEDY RIDE TO PUEBLO DE LOS ANGELES! HA HA HA HA!** ULP! WHAP
SO MUCH FOR MONASTARIO AND HIS MEN TONIGHT, TORNADO! AND NOW, BACK TO THE CHURCH!	LATER... **I-I HEARD ALL THE NOISE, SEÑOR! BUT I THOUGHT I'D STAY INSIDE! WHAT...WHAT WAS IT ALL ABOUT!** **IT WAS ZORRO! ZORRO, HIMSELF! HE WAS TRULY MAGNIFICENT! YOU SHOULD HAVE SEEN HIM!**
I'M-ER-SORRY I COULDN'T BE OF HELP, BUT-ER-I DON'T LIKE VIOLENCE! **YOU ARE RIGHT, MY SON! WE SHOULD NOT, AFTER ALL, CONDONE THIS VIOLENCE!**	**WE CAN'T HELP BUT ADMIRE ZORRO, BUT PERHAPS IT WOULD BE BETTER IF WE WERE ALL MORE LIKE YOU, DON DIEGO! YOU HAVE SUCH A QUIET AND PEACEFUL LIFE!**

WALT DISNEY PRESENTS
Zorro
"Ghost of the Mission", part two..
EARLY MORNING IN THE COURTYARD...
LOOK, MI CAPITAN! THE SOLDIERS FOUND HIM SLEEPING NEAR THE ROAD...BEHIND SOME ROCKS!
A MISSION INDIAN! HA! HE MUST HAVE BEEN TOO WEAK TO RUN FAR! MAYBE I CAN GET SOME INFORMATION OUT OF HIM!
FORGIVE ME, COMANDANTE! BUT THIS INDIAN WILL NEVER BETRAY HIS OWN PEOPLE!
OH, NO? THERE ARE WAYS, SERGEANT! HE HAS A FAMILY HIDING OUT THERE SOMEWHERE IN THE HILLS! NO DOUBT HE WANTS TO SEE THEM AGAIN!
I AM TAKING YOU BACK TO THE MISSION, WRETCH! WHATEVER I TELL THE PADRE, DO NOT OPEN YOUR MOUTH TO DENY IT! OR YOU WILL NEVER SEE YOUR FAMILY AGAIN! UNDERSTAND?
Y-YES! I...I WILL N-NOT SPEAK..!
ORDER THE LANCERS OUT, GARCIA! WE'RE RIDING FOR KING AND COUNTRY AGAINST THE HOSTILE RED SAVAGES!
RED SAVAGES? ER...SI', MI CAPITAN!
WHILE IN DON DIEGO de la VEGA'S BEDROOM...
NOW WATCH ME AGAIN, BERNARDO! IT IS VERY SIMPLE! THE FINGERS SO...!
PLINK PLINK
CONTINUED...

NOW YOU TRY IT! YOU MUST LEARN TO PLAY SO YOU CAN COVER FOR ME WHEN I AM OUT RIDING AS ZORRO! OTHERWISE, FATHER MAY GROW SUSPICIOUS!	PLUNK TWANNNG NOT GOOD, BERNARDO! BUT YOU MUST NOT GIVE UP! NOW I MUST RIDE TO THE MISSION TO SEE IF SEÑOR TORRES HAS GOTTEN SAFELY AWAY!
LATER... HOW SAD THE MISSION LOOKS NOW! NO INDIANS! NOT EVEN AN ANIMAL IN SIGHT!	AH, DIEGO! I AM GLAD IT IS YOU! I WAS AFRAID CAPITAN MONASTARIO MIGHT HAVE RETURNED! ARE THE INDIANS STILL HIDING IN THE HILLS, PADRE?
YES, BUT THEY WILL COME BACK WHEN THE DANGER IS OVER! I HAVE KEPT SEÑOR TORRES HERE, THOUGH! I AM AFRAID THE SOLDIERS ARE STILL WAITING TO SEIZE HIM IF HE LEAVES! THAT IS WISE, PADRE! BUT HE SHOULDN'T WAIT TOO LONG TO SET OUT FOR MONTEREY!	IT IS MONASTARIO AGAIN! AND HIS LANCERS! THEY MUST PLAN TO TAKE TORRES BY FORCE! LOOK! THE CAPITAN ALSO HAS ONE OF THE MISSION INDIANS!

GARCIA! POST SENTRIES AND KEEP A SHARP WATCH! THE PRISONER COMES WITH ME!

INOCENTE! WHAT HAVE THEY DONE TO YOU?

CAREFUL, PADRE! HE'S A DANGEROUS SAVAGE WHO'S CONFESSED THAT HIS PEOPLE ARE PLANNING TO BURN THE MISSION AND ROB YOU!

THE INDIANS ARE LIKE MY CHILDREN! THIS CANNOT BE TRUE! INOCENTE, SPEAK UP! DON'T BE AFRAID!

I-I...!

YOU SEE, HE WON'T DENY IT! I HAVE NO CHOICE BUT TO PUT THIS MISSION UNDER *MARTIAL LAW*, PADRE!

IT IS A TRICK! A SHABBY TRICK!

IT'S FOR YOUR OWN PROTECTION, PADRE! THIS MISSION IS UNDER MY COMMAND! YOU WILL PROVIDE FOOD AND SHELTER FOR MY LANCERS, TOO!

AND NOW, I SHALL *SELECT* A PRIVATE ROOM FOR MY HEADQUARTERS!

IT'S QUITE OBVIOUS THAT THE CAPITAN IS UNABLE TO GET TORRES ANY OTHER WAY, SO HE HAS INVENTED A FALSE INDIAN UPRISING AS HIS EXCUSE TO TAKE OVER THE MISSION!

AS LONG AS TORRES REMAINS INSIDE THE CHURCH, HE IS STILL PROTECTED BY HOLY SANCTUARY, PADRE!

TRUE! BUT CAPITAN MONASTARIO WILL KEEP HIM IN THERE! HOW LONG CAN HE LIVE WITHOUT FOOD OR WATER?

WELL, I SHALL GO AND TELL MY FATHER WHAT HAS OCCURRED! HE HAS A KNOWLEDGE OF THE LAW! PERHAPS HE CAN HELP! ER...YES... PERHAPS!	LATER... BERNARDO! YOUR PLAYING HAS IMPROVED A LITTLE! SOON YOU WILL LOCK YOURSELF IN MY ROOM AND PLAY THE GUITAR UNTIL I RETURN!
ZORRO MUST RIDE AGAIN TONIGHT, AND RETURN WITHOUT MY FATHER MISSING ME! GO AND HAVE THE COOK PREPARE PLENTY OF FOOD TO PACK IN MY SADDLE BAG!	THAT NIGHT... SOLDIERS EVERYWHERE...! BUT I'VE GOT TO GET FOOD AND WATER TO SEÑOR TORRES! ONE MOMENT, PADRE! I THOUGHT YOU MIGHT TRY SOMETHING LIKE THIS!
YOU CAN'T KEEP ME FROM GOING INTO MY OWN CHURCH! NO, BUT I CANNOT ALLOW YOU TO CARRY FOOD AND DRINK TO A TRAITOR! LET ME HAVE THAT!	MM-M-M VERY APPETIZING! I THINK I'LL ENJOY THIS, PADRE! YOU ARE INHUMAN! BEWARE, LEST AN ESPECIALLY WARM SPOT BE RESERVED FOR YOU IN THE HEREAFTER!

At that minute, behind the mission...

EASY, TORNADO! I'VE GOT TO GET THIS FOOD TO SEÑOR TORRES!

THERE'S OUR ALERT SENTRY, SERGEANT GARCIA! HE WILL GIVE US NO TROUBLE! HE SLEEPS SOUNDLY!

ZZZZz

Zorro slips silently into the church...

PSSST! SEÑOR TORRES! QUIET! HERE IS FOOD AND WATER!

Z-ZORRO

THANK YOU, SEÑOR ZORRO! AGAIN YOU RISK YOUR LIFE TO HELP ME!

Suddenly...

AHA! SEÑOR ZORRO! YOU CANNOT CLAIM SANCTUARY! AT LAST I HAVE YOU!

YOU CAN'T FIGHT IN THE CHURCH, ZORRO! ESCAPE IF YOU CAN!

Knowing he cannot resort to force within the church, Zorro heads for the tower...

HA! THE GREAT ZORRO HAS TRAPPED HIMSELF!

LET HIM GET TO THE BELFRY! HE CAN GO NO FURTHER!
NOW—IF MY PLAN WORKS!
ZORRO REACHES THE BELFRY AND LEAPS OUT...
THERE HE IS!
SO! THEN ZORRO IS AT THE END OF HIS ROPE! HA HA HA!
THERE!
ADIOS, SEÑOR ZORRO!
GARCIA! ZORRO IS WOUNDED! HE'S DROPPED INTO THE CHURCHYARD! GET HIM!
O-O-O-O-F! ...GOT TO... GET AWAY FROM HERE!

BUT FIRST... IT MIGHT BE WISE TO SLOW UP THE SERGEANT AND HIS MEN!	SWIFTLY, ZORRO SETS A SNARE... THIS OUGHT TO DO IT!
OOOWWWW OOOFFF — YOUR FEET ARE TOO BIG, SERGEANT! HA HA HA HA!	WHAT...? YOU IDIOTS! ZORRO HAS OUTWITTED YOU AGAIN! AFTER HIM! BUT, MI CAPITAN, IT WAS THIS WAY! I—!
SOME TIME LATER, IN DIEGO'S ROOM, BERNARDO'S STRUMMING CONTINUES... KNOCK! KNOCK! DIEGO! STOP THAT INFERNAL NOISE AND OPEN THIS DOOR! TWANG TWINNG	DIEGO! WHAT'S THE MATTER WITH YOU? UNLOCK THE DOOR! YES, FATHER! KNOCK KNO!

QUICKLY, BERNARDO! GET UNDER THE BED! **KNOCK KNOCK**	ARE YOU GETTING DEAF, DIEGO? AND THAT TERRIBLE MUSIC... HOW CAN I SLEEP? / I'M SORRY, FATHER! I WAS ENGROSSED IN COMPOSING A NEW SONG!
PLEASE STOP, DIEGO! I DON'T UNDERSTAND YOU! ALL YOU THINK OF IS LITERATURE, MUSIC, PAINTING... / THAT IS MY LIFE, FATHER! JUST AS YOURS IS RAISING CATTLE AND BREEDING HORSES!	LATER... YOU DID WELL, BERNARDO! BUT *ZORRO* DID *NOT!* THERE WERE TOO MANY SOLDIERS! DON NACHO TORRES WILL HAVE TO WAIT A WHILE LONGER FOR FREEDOM!
EARLY NEXT DAY, IN THE MISSION COURTYARD... SERGEANT GARCIA! SEÑOR DE LA VEGA REQUESTS YOUR PERMISSION TO SEE THE PADRE! / OH? AND WHAT IS THE PURPOSE OF THIS VISIT?	I HAVE AN OLD MANUSCRIPT, SERGEANT, THAT PADRE FELIPE EXPRESSED A DESIRE TO SEE! / MANUSCRIPT, EH? AND WHAT IS THIS STRANGE WRITING ALL OVER IT?

IT IS LATIN! AN ACCOUNT OF SOMETHING STRANGE THAT HAPPENED HERE MANY YEARS AGO! I DON'T THINK YOU'D BE INTERESTED! / SOMETHING STRANGE? WHAT WAS IT?	WELL, I DON'T KNOW AS THERE'S MUCH TRUTH IN IT, ALTHOUGH THIS DOCUMENT SEEMS AUTHENTIC ENOUGH! YOU SEE, THIS ALL HAPPENED BACK IN 1771, WHEN THE MISSION WAS FIRST BUILT! / YES? YES?
A BAND OF MARAUDING SAVAGES STRUCK IN THE DEAD OF NIGHT! ONE MISSION MONK WAS KILLED... RIGHT AT THIS VERY SPOT... / THIS VERY SPOT...?	YES! AND EVER SINCE, HIS GHOST HAS HAUNTED THE MISSION ON DARK MOONLESS NIGHTS! / A—A GHOST? BUT WH-WHAT DOES IT LOOK LIKE?
A FIGURE IN A COWLED ROBE! IT APPEARS IN THE CHURCHYARD AND WALKS THROUGH THE EMPTY CORRIDORS, MOANING! AND WHEN THE CHURCH BELL RINGS AT THE SAME TIME, IT IS A DIRE WARNING! / A—A WARNING?	YES! WHOEVER COMES FACE TO FACE WITH THE GHOST WILL DIE! BUT SURELY YOU DO NOT BELIEVE THESE THINGS, SERGEANT! NOW I MUST SEE THE PADRE! / ER...YES, OF COURSE, GO RIGHT IN, DIEGO!

Panel 1:
DIEGO! WHAT DO YOU HAVE?
JUST A MANUSCRIPT, PADRE! A PRETEXT TO SEE YOU! HOW IS DON NACHO? AND THE INDIAN?

Panel 2:
DON NACHO IS QUITE DEJECTED! AND THE INDIAN IS TIED UP IN THE STONE BODEGA, BEHIND THE PEPPER TREE! I FEAR THE WORST, DIEGO!
DO NOT DESPAIR, PADRE! SOMEHOW, I FEEL THAT THIS REIGN OF TERROR WILL SOON COME TO AN END!

Panel 3:
THAT NIGHT...
SERGEANT! WHAT OF THIS STRANGE TALE YOU HAVE BEEN TELLING EVERYBODY! THIS GHOST! WHAT DO YOU MAKE OF IT?
BAH! IT IS A FOOLISH TALE MEANT FOR OLD WOMEN WHO COULD BELIEVE SUCH NONSENSE!

Panel 4:
WELL, IT IS A MOONLESS NIGHT, AND THE HOUR IS ALMOST MIDNIGHT! TELL ME THE STORY AGAIN, GARCIA! I LIKE...!

Panel 5:
BONNNNNG
TH-THE CH-CHURCH BELL!
YI-I-I-I-I!

Panel 6:
CONTRERAS! WHY DID YOU SOUND THE ALARM?
I DIDN'T RING THE BELL, SERGEANT! IT RINGS BY ITSELF!
BONNNNNG

Panel 1: LOOK! SOMETHING IS MOVING IN THE CHURCHYARD! / YI!!!!!!!! IT IS THE GHOST!	**Panel 2:** WHAT'S GOING ON HERE? / IT'S...IT'S THE...THE GHOST, MI CAPITAN! WE MUST RUN!
Panel 3: BAH! GHOSTS AND PHANTOMS DO NOT EXIST! COME WITH ME SERGEANT! WE'LL FIND OUT WHO'S PLAYING THIS LITTLE JOKE! / BUT...BUT... MI CAPITAN! LOOK! THERE IT IS AGAIN!	**Panel 4:** AFTER IT! / IT'S GOING INTO THE BARRACKS!
Panel 5: YEEOWW! IT'S THE GHOST OF THE MONK! / LET ME OUT OF HERE! / COME BACK! COME BACK, YOU DESERTERS!	**Panel 6:** SH-SHALL I GO AFTER THEM, SIR? / COWARD! NO! — YOU WILL HELP ME CATCH THIS FALSE PHANTOM! THERE HE IS NOW!

HE WENT BEHIND THAT TREE! NOW WE'VE GOT HIM!	BUT TH-THAT'S THE TREE WHERE THE... THE MONK WAS KILLED...!

TH-THERE IS NO ONE HERE! BUT HOW...?	YOU SEE, THE LEGEND *IS* TRUE! IT J-JUST DISAPPEARED INTO THIN AIR!

BUT A FEW FEET OVER THEIR HEADS...

AHA! YOU ARE IN A GOOD SPOT, MI CAPITAN! JUST STAND THERE FOR A MOMENT AND...!

THE DISGUISED ZORRO'S AIM IS TRUE...

SWISH RIP BONK

THE CURSE H-HAS C-COME TRUE!

YI-I-I-I-I-I!

I THINK THE MAD GHOST HAS SERVED ITS PURPOSE WELL! NOW TO FINISH THIS NIGHT'S WORK!

YOU ARE FREE, INOCENTE!

SEÑOR ZORRO! AGAIN I THANK YOU!

Panel 1
"STOP! STOP, ZORRO! YOU ARE BEHIND ALL THIS! MY SOLDIERS HAVE ALL DESERTED!"

"AND GARCIA, TOO, CAPITAN! YOU HAD BETTER START ROUNDING THEM UP! ADIOS!"

Panel 2
FURTHER OUT ON THE TRAIL...

"AH, BERNARDO! YOU DID A GOOD JOB OF RINGING THE CHURCHBELL WITH YOUR SLINGSHOT! AND NOW LET'S RIDE! BACK TO THE HACIENDA!"

Panel 3
AND BACK AT THE MISSION...

"BUT ARE YOU SURE IT IS SAFE FOR ME TO COME OUT OF THE CHURCH, PADRE FELIPE?"

"YES, TORRES! EVERY SOLDIER IS GONE! AND I HAVE LOCKED THE COMANDANTE OUT FOR THE NIGHT!"

Panel 4
"SO DINE IN PEACE! SOON YOU MUST SET OUT FOR MONTEREY!"

"BUT WHAT FRIGHTENED THE SOLDIERS AWAY? I SAW NOTHING!"

Panel 5
"YOU MIGHT CALL IT AN OLD LEGEND, DON NACHO! BUT I PREFER TO CALL IT A NEW MIRACLE... A MIRACLE CALLED ZORRO!"

WALT DISNEY Presents ZORRO

GARCIA'S SECRET

AS DAWN BREAKS OVER THE CUARTEL COURTYARD IN THE VILLAGE OF LOS ANGELES, A SLEEPY-EYED LANCER EMERGES FROM THE BARRACKS, A FOLDED FLAG BENEATH HIS ARM. BUT SUDDENLY HE REALIZES THAT ALL IS NOT AS IT SHOULD BE...

Z-ZORRO! IT IS ZORRO!

SERGEANT GARCIA! COME QUICK! ZORRO ...THE FLAG... IT'S...IT'S...!

UH...WHAT'S THAT?... ZORRO? FLAG? WHAT ARE YOU TALKING ABOUT?

THERE! LOOK UP THERE ON THE FLAGPOLE!

10169-712
W.D. ZORRO #8 - 679

69

HOLA! ZORRO HAS BEEN HERE DURING THE NIGHT! SOMETHING TOLD ME NOT TO GET UP THIS MORNING! / IT WAS ONLY A FEW MINUTES AGO, SERGEANT! I JUST SAW HIM GOING OVER THE WALL!	WELL, DON'T JUST STAND THERE! TAKE IT DOWN QUICKLY... BEFORE THE CAPITAN SEES IT! / BUT...BUT THE ROPE IS GONE, SERGEANT! I THINK THE FLAG IS NAILED UP THERE!
BAH! ALWAYS EXCUSES! STAND BACK! I WILL CLIMB THE POLE AND GET THE FLAG MYSELF! / CLIMB...UP THERE...?	OOOOOOF
BAH! THAT ZORRO AND HIS TRICKS! HE HAS GREASED THE POLE! / BUT IT COULDN'T BE GREASED ALL THE WAY! PERHAPS IF YOU JUMPED HIGHER...!	I HAVE A BETTER IDEA! BEND DOWN SO I CAN GET ON YOUR SHOULDERS! / UH...WELL... IF I MUST...!

71

Panel 1:
SERGEANT GARCIA! WHAT IS THE MEANING OF THIS? HOW DID THAT FLAG GET UP THERE?
ULP...!

Panel 2:
HA HA HO HO HA HA HA HA

Panel 3:
I AM SORRY, MI CAPITAN! WE WERE...TRYING TO...GET IT DOWN, BUT...
YOU SHOULD HAVE HAD IT DOWN SOONER! YOU'RE MAKING US A LAUGHINGSTOCK OF THE WHOLE PUEBLO!

Panel 4:
THOSE VAGABONDS THAT LAUGHED...**ARREST** THEM! I'LL TEACH THEM NOT TO MOCK MY AUTHORITY!
YES, CAPITAN!

Panel 5:
SO! ZORRO PLACES A FLAG OF VICTORY OVER MY CUARTEL, AND YOU THINK IT IS AMUSING, EH?
OH, NO, COMANDANTE! WE WERE NOT LAUGHING AT THAT!

Panel 6:
SILENCE! YOU ARE UNDER ARREST! AND I BELIEVE I HAVE SOMETHING IN MIND THAT WILL KEEP YOU OUT OF TROUBLE FOR A WHILE!
BUT, COMANDANTE, OUR WIVES AND CHILDREN WILL GO HUNGRY!

THE STABLE ROOF NEEDS REPAIRING! IF YOU CAN DO THIS BY SUNSET TOMORROW, YOU CAN GO BACK TO YOUR FAMILIES! LET ME SEE, IT WILL REQUIRE ABOUT THIRTY BUCKETS OF PITCH, WHICH YOU MAY BRING FROM THE TAR PITS!

IT IS IMPOSSIBLE, COMANDANTE! THE TAR PITS ARE MILES FROM HERE! EVEN IF YOU GAVE US A WAGON AND MEN TO HELP, WE COULD NOT...!

I WILL GIVE YOU NOTHING BUT SIXTY LASHES AND SIXTY DAYS IF THE JOB ISN'T FINISHED IN TIME!...TAKE THEM AWAY, SENTRY!

AS FOR YOU, GARCIA, I GIVE YOU TWO MINUTES TO REMOVE THAT FLAG! TWO MINUTES, UNDERSTAND?

Y-YES, MI CAPITAN!

I WILL GET IT DOWN! CORPORAL, BRING ME AN AXE!

MINUTES LATER...

HERE IS THE ZORRO FLAG, CAPITAN! I CUT THE FLAGPOLE DOWN TO GET IT!

WHAT? CUT THE FLAGPOLE DOWN? GARCIA, YOU ARE MORE STUPID THAN I THOUGHT! I OUGHT TO HAVE YOU DISHONORABLY DISCHARGED FROM SERVICE!

WAIT! THAT MIGHT BE AN EXCELLENT IDEA! YES... I WILL HAVE YOU DISMISSED!

DISMISSED? BUT...BUT...

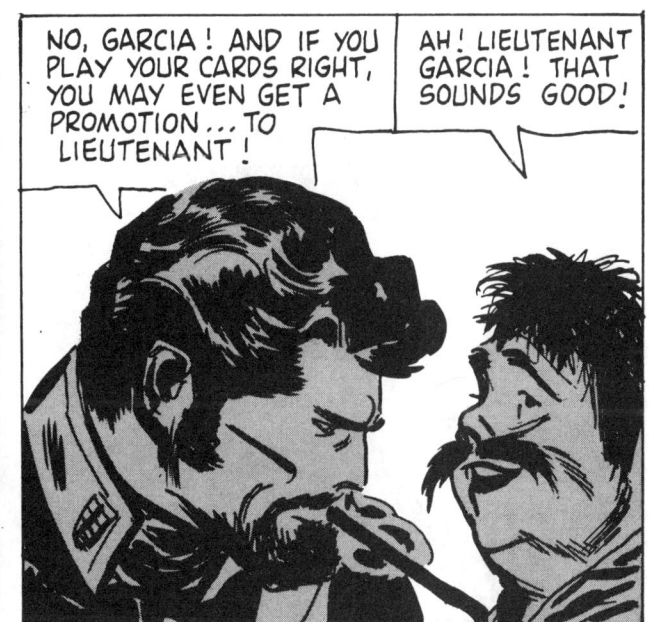

Panel 1:
"YES, YOU WILL BE PUBLICLY DISGRACED! STRIPPED OF YOUR RANK! THEN YOU CAN MINGLE WITH THE COMMON PEOPLE! THEY PROTECT ZORRO... YOU MAY FIND OUT WHERE ZORRO HIDES!"

"OH...UH...I SEE! YOU ARE NOT *REALLY* DISMISSING ME....I *THINK*!"

Panel 2:
"NO, GARCIA! AND IF YOU PLAY YOUR CARDS RIGHT, YOU MAY EVEN GET A PROMOTION...TO LIEUTENANT!"

"AH! LIEUTENANT GARCIA! THAT SOUNDS GOOD!"

Panel 3:
MUCH LATER THAT AFTERNOON...

"BUENOS DIAS, SEÑOR ALCADE! WHAT IS THE MEANING OF THE CROWD NEAR THE CUARTEL?"

"HAVE YOU NOT HEARD, DIEGO? SERGEANT GARCIA HAS JUST BEEN DRUMMED OUT OF THE SERVICE! A PUBLIC COURT-MARTIAL!"

Panel 4:
"IT IS TOO BAD WE ARE LATE! I WOULD LIKED TO HAVE SEEN THAT FOR MYSELF!"

"BE CAREFUL, SEÑOR!"

Panel 5:
"IT'S JUST THAT WE DO NOT WANT TO SPILL A DROP, SEÑOR! IT HAS TAKEN US HALF A DAY TO GET THESE BUCKETS FILLED AT THE TAR PITS!"

"THE TAR PITS? BUT WHERE ARE YOU TAKING TAR IN SUCH A HURRY?"

Panel 6:
"TO REPAIR THE STABLE ROOF FOR THE COMANDANTE BY TOMORROW SUNSET... OR WE WILL GET SIXTY LASHES!"

"IT IS TERRIBLE, SEÑOR! WE DID NOTHING BUT LAUGH AT THE FAT SERGEANT WHEN HE TRIED TO GET ZORRO'S FLAG DOWN!"

"THIS IS BAD, BERNARDO! I CANNOT ALLOW THESE INNOCENT MEN TO SUFFER BECAUSE OF MY PRANKS! PERHAPS IF I TALKED TO GARCIA..."	DIEGO FINDS THE APPARENTLY DEJECTED GARCIA IN THE TAVERN... "AH, THERE YOU ARE, GARCIA! MIND IF I JOIN YOU?" "OF COURSE NOT... IF YOU DON'T MIND SITTING WITH A MISERABLE EX-SERGEANT!"
"NO ONE ELSE WILL EVEN TALK WITH ME NOW! BUT AT LEAST I AM GLAD I DO NOT HAVE TO DO THE COMANDANTE'S DIRTY WORK FOR HIM ANYMORE!" "YOU MUST BE CAREFUL WHAT YOU SAY ABOUT OUR COMANDANTE, GARCIA!"	"WHAT DO I CARE? I SHALL BE A BEGGAR...A VAGRANT ...AND END UP IN JAIL... UNLESS...UNLESS I KNEW WHERE TO FIND THIS ZORRO! HE WOULD HELP ME!" "ZORRO! THE OUTLAW! SURELY YOU CANNOT MEAN THAT!"
"AH, DON DIEGO! WELCOME! WHAT IS YOUR PLEASURE?" "ER...MERELY A REQUEST, TIO! HAVE YOU NO POSITION THAT MY FRIEND GARCIA MIGHT FILL?"	"WELL, ER...IF HE IS A FRIEND OF YOURS, DON DIEGO, I MIGHT... ER...POSSIBLY USE HIM! THAT IS, IF HE IS WILLING TO WORK FOR FOOD AND SLEEPING QUARTERS!" "NOW THAT SOUNDS LIKE A GRACIOUS OFFER TO ME! WHAT DO YOU SAY, GARCIA? NOW YOU HAVE A JOB!"

Panel 1:
"WELL, IT WILL ONLY BE TEMPORARY, DIEGO! I'VE MADE UP MY MIND! AS SOON AS I CAN, I AM GOING TO JOIN FORCES WITH ZORRO! I WILL GET EVEN WITH THE COMANDANTE!"
"AH, THEN I WISH YOU LUCK!"

Panel 2: *Late that night, Garcia is busy cleaning the tavern and not liking his job too well...*
"THIS IS A MUCH BIGGER TAVERN THAN I THOUGHT, SEÑOR TIO!"
"WELL, AFTER YOU'RE FINISHED HERE, YOU MAY BRING IN WOOD FOR THE MORNING FIRE, SCOUR THE POTS, AND CLEAN THE LAMPS!"

Panel 3:
"THEN, AFTER YOU HAVE SCRUBBED THE KITCHEN FLOOR, YOU MAY GO TO BED! THERE IS A COT AT THE BACK ENTRANCE! BUENOS NOCHES!"
"(ULP)...Y-YES, SEÑOR!"

Panel 4: *Minutes later...*
"GOOD EVENING, GARCIA! I HAVE HEARD THAT YOU WISHED TO BE MY FRIEND!"
"WH-WHAT...?"

Panel 5:
"MAKE NO NOISE, GARCIA! I WISH TO KNOW THE REASON FOR THIS SUDDEN CHANGE OF HEART OF YOURS!"
"Z-ZORRO! YOU... YOU MUST BELIEVE ME...! I SEE THINGS DIFFERENTLY NOW!"

Panel 6:
"I UNDERSTAND NOW WHY YOU HAVE FOUGHT AGAINST MONASTARIO! I, TOO, WISH TO PUNISH HIM FOR HIS CRIMES! I CAN HELP YOU, ZORRO! I AM AN EXCELLENT HORSEMAN...A GOOD SWORDSMAN...WELL, REASONABLY GOOD!"

Panel 1:
H-M-M! PERHAPS I SHALL TEST THIS NEWLY-FOUND PURITY...! MEET ME AT DAWN AT THE SIGNPOST OF THE LA BREA RANCHO!

YOU MEAN... THE ONE NEAR THE TAR PITS?

Panel 2:
THAT'S RIGHT! WILL I EXPECT YOU?

YES! YES! I WILL BE THERE! AT DAWN!

Panel 3:
After waiting a short time to make sure Zorro has left, Garcia hurries to the Cuartel...

HOW DARE YOU AWAKEN ME AT THIS TIME OF NIGHT! WHAT DO YOU WANT?

YOUR PLAN WORKED, CAPITAN! I HAVE JUST SEEN ZORRO AT THE TAVERN! HE WANTS ME TO MEET HIM AT DAWN!

Panel 4:
AH! GOOD! THEN ZORRO IS TAKING YOU INTO HIS CONFIDENCE! BUT WHERE ARE YOU TO MEET HIM?

AT THE SIGNPOST OF THE LA BREA RANCHO! WE WILL CAPTURE ZORRO, AND THEN I SHALL BECOME A LIEUTENANT, EH, CAPITAN?

Panel 5:
PERHAPS! BUT NOW RETURN TO THE TAVERN! USE ONE OF THEIR HORSES AT DAWN! I SHALL FOLLOW WITH A COMPANY OF LANCERS!

YES, CAPITAN! ZORRO WILL BE PLENTY SURPRISED!

Panel 6:
OH, GARCIA! TELL THE CORPORAL THAT I SHALL LEAVE THE ORDERS OF THE DAY ON MY DESK!

GOOD! I'VE LEARNED ALL I NEED TO KNOW!

DAWN FINDS PEPE AND PANCHO AT THE TAR PITS, STILL WEARILY TRYING TO CARRY OUT MONASTARIO'S ORDERS... "BE CAREFUL, PEPE! DO NOT FALL IN, FOR I AM TOO TIRED TO PULL YOU OUT!" "WHAT IS THE USE? WE CAN NEVER FINISH BY SUNSET!"	"LOOK! THERE IS THE FAT SERGEANT WE LAUGHED AT! WHAT COULD HE BE DOING HERE?" "HE LOOKS HAPPY, INDEED! PERHAPS IT IS BECAUSE HE WAS THROWN OUT OF THE ARMY!"
MINUTES LATER... "DUCK DOWN! THE COMANDANTE AND SOME OF HIS MEN! I WONDER IF THEY ARE AFTER THE SERGEANT?" "QUIÉN SABE? THEY WILL BE AFTER *US* IF THEY SEE WE ARE NOT BUSILY AT WORK!"	REACHING THE SIGNPOST, GARCIA FINDS ONLY A NOTE WAITING FOR HIM... "H-M-M! FROM ZORRO! I'D BETTER CALL THE CAPITAN!" *Rancho La Brea*
"WELL? WHERE IS ZORRO?" "HE LEFT THIS NOTE, MI CAPITAN! IT SAYS TO PROCEED AT ONCE TO THE SUMMIT OF SAN VICENTE ROCK!"	"WELL, WHAT ARE YOU WAITING FOR, THEN? RIDE THERE! WE WILL BE BEHIND YOU!" "YES, CAPITAN! BUT IT IS A *LONG* WAY...!"

MUCH LATER, GARCIA IS THE FIRST TO REACH SAN VICENTE ROCK...

SEÑOR COMANDANTE, DO I HAVE TO CLIMB WAY UP THERE? IT IS SO STEEP!

FOLLOW HIS INSTRUCTIONS! HE MUST BE UP THERE! PERHAPS HE WANTED TO MEET YOU IN A MORE SECRETIVE PLACE THAN THE TAR PITS!

BAH! THIS SECRET MISSION TO CATCH ZORRO IS MUCH HARDER WORK THAN I EXPECTED!

HURRY, GARCIA! WE WILL BE RIGHT BEHIND YOU!

BUT, AS MONASTARIO AND HIS MEN START UP AFTER GARCIA...

COMANDANTE...I...I D-DON'T KNOW H-HOW TO TELL YOU...! IT...MUST HAVE BEEN A TRICK! ZORRO IS...NOT HERE!

WHAT? YOU IDIOT, BRINGING US ON A WILD-GOOSE CHASE! FOR THIS, I WILL THROW YOU OUT OF THE ARMY!

ZORRO IS WISE TO US! FOR SOME REASON, HE WANTED US AWAY FROM THE CUARTEL! HE'S PROBABLY BURNING THE BARRACKS! TO YOUR HORSES, QUICKLY!

BACK IN THE COURTYARD OF THE CUARTEL, THE CORPORAL HAS READ THE ORDERS FOR THE DAY...

THAT'S STRANGE! THE COMANDANTE WANTS ME TO PUT EVERY BUCKET IN THE CUARTEL INTO HIS CARRIAGE AND TAKE THEM TO THE TAR PITS, WHERE I WILL RECEIVE FURTHER ORDERS!

WELL, ORDERS ARE ORDERS!

AND SOON, ON THE DUSTY ROAD THAT LEADS TO THE TAR PITS...

THAT'S THE COMANDANTE'S COACH! I WONDER WHAT'S GOING ON?

WHO CARES? WE'VE STILL GOT TO GET THIS TAR TO LOS ANGELES!

THEN THE COACH REACHES THE TAR PITS...
VERY GOOD, CORPORAL! I SEE YOU READ THE NOTE I SUBSTITUTED FOR THE COMANDANTE'S ORDERS FOR THE DAY!
WH-WHAT? ZORRO!
THAT'S RIGHT! NOW TAKE THE BUCKETS OUT AND FILL THEM WITH PITCH! EVERY ONE OF THEM!
WHATEVER YOU SAY, SEÑOR ZORRO!
SOME TIME LATER...
YOU ARE A FAST WORKER, CORPORAL! THAT'S THE LAST BUCKET TO FILL! NOW YOU MAY DRIVE BACK TO THE CUARTEL! AND I SUGGEST THAT YOU HURRY AS THE COMANDANTE WOULDN'T LIKE IT IF HE KNEW YOU USED HIS CARRIAGE TO HAUL PITCH!
YOU... YOU WOULDN'T TELL HIM, WOULD YOU?
WHEN YOU GET BACK, FINISH REPAIRING THE STABLE ROOF... AND I SHALL KEEP YOUR SECRET! ADIOS, AMIGO!
AND NOW, MONASTARIO AND HIS MEN SHOULD BE RETURNING THIS WAY SOON FROM THEIR LONG RIDE! PERHAPS I CAN RIG A LITTLE SURPRISE FOR THEM!
JUST A FEW BUSHES ALONG THE BANK, AND THE TAR PIT WILL BE COMPLETELY HIDDEN FROM THIS SIDE!

NOT FAR FROM THE LA BREA RANCHO SIGNPOST...

CAPITAN! CAN WE NOT REST ONCE MORE? MY HORSE IS READY TO DROP!

ALL RIGHT, BUT NOT FOR LONG! THAT ZORRO IS UP TO SOMETHING TO MAKE ME LOOK RIDICULOUS!

HOLA, CAPITAN!

WH-WHAT'S THAT?

ZORRO! AFTER HIM!

YES, CAPITAN! AND I AM GOING TO LEAD YOU A MERRY CHASE!

AH! I'M HIDDEN BY TREES! NOW TO SKIRT THE TAR PIT AND WAIT ON THE OTHER SIDE!

HE HEADED INTO THAT CLUMP OF TREES! CLOSE IN ON HIM!

AHA! MAYBE I WILL BE A LIEUTENANT, AFTER ALL!

80

YOU ARE SLOW, COMANDANTE! ARE YOUR HORSES TIRED?
I WILL SHOW YOU HOW TIRED THEY ARE! ...LANCERS...CHARGE!
YIIIIEEEE
WHAT IS IT, CAPITAN?
YIIPE!!
(ULP!) A TAR PIT!
HA! HA! HA! ANYBODY ELSE FOR A SWIM?
PULL ME OUT OF HERE YOU IDIOTS! **PULL ME OUT!**
M-ME, TOO!
FAREWELL, CAPITAN! UNTIL WE MEET AGAIN!
(GULP!) THAT ZORRO!.. I'LL...I'LL...GET HIM FOR THIS!

LOOK OUT, YOU IDIOTS! (ULP!)
YI-YI-YI-YIYIEE
LATER, BACK IN THE PLAZA, NEAR THE CUARTEL...
CAPITAN MONASTARIO! I JUST SAW YOUR STABLE ROOF COVERED WITH NEW PITCH! SUCH A FINE JOB... AND I SEE THAT YOU HAVE BEEN WORKING ON IT, TOO!
YOU ARE NOT VERY AMUSING, SEÑOR DE LA VEGA!
AND SERGEANT GARCIA! CONGRATULATIONS! I SEE YOU ARE BACK IN THE FOLD! IT IS WHERE YOU REALLY BELONG! NO?
THIS IS NOT THE MOMENT TO CONGRATULATE ME, DON DIEGO! SOME OTHER TIME, PLEASE!
GUARDS! HEAT WATER! PLENTY OF IT! AND CLOSE THOSE GATES BEHIND YOU!
THERE ARE PANCHO AND PEPE LEAVING THE CUARTEL! THE CAPITAN HAS NO FURTHER REASON TO HOLD THEM!
YES, I SEE IT, BERNARDO! THE LETTER "Z" HAS BEEN PRINTED ON EACH GATE! AND IN BLACK TAR!
H-M-M! LOOKS LIKE ZORRO MAY HAVE BEEN AROUND HERE SOMEWHERE, EH, BERNARDO? BUT NOW, LET'S GET BACK TO THE HACIENDA! I COULD USE SOME SLEEP!
Z Z

Walt Disney Presents ZORRO
THE KING'S EMISSARY

An unusual sight greets the townspeople... Don Diego de la Vega is being escorted under guard...

One moment! What is wrong, Diego?

Your pardon, Señor Alcade! It is not permitted to speak to the prisoner!

Prisoner? What is Señor de la Vega charged with?

A sergeant is not supposed to know anything, your honor! I just follow orders!

You are well qualified for your rank, sergeant!

Please, Don Diego, we have no time for small talk! We must report to Capitan Monastario!

By all means! We mustn't keep the Comandante waiting! Hasta la vista, my friend!

Panel 1: HERE IS SEÑOR DIEGO DE LA VEGA, MI CAPITAN, AS ORDERED!

GOOD! SERGEANT, CLOSE THE DOOR BEHIND YOU! WHAT I HAVE TO SAY IS OF GREAT INTEREST TO YOU, TOO!

Panel 2: I HAVE HERE A LONG LIST OF ZORRO'S OFFENSES, AND ONE VERY INTERESTING FACT HAS STRUCK ME, SEÑOR DE LA VEGA!

I LIKE INTERESTING FACTS, CAPITAN!

Panel 3: YOU MAY NOT LIKE THIS! EVERY TIME ZORRO HAS STRUCK, YOU WERE CLOSE AT HAND! BUT WHEN HE ACTUALLY APPEARED, YOU WERE NEVER SEEN! HOW DO YOU EXPLAIN *THAT*?

THAT IS EASY, CAPITAN! DON DIEGO IS AFRAID! AFTER ALL, HE IS NOT A SOLDIER! HE IS A SCHOLAR!

Panel 4: BAH! HIS DISGUISE AS A SCHOLAR IS *TOO* GOOD! HE *IS ZORRO*!

Panel 5: HO! HO! HA! SEÑOR COMANDANTE, IN ALL OF CALIFORNIA, NO MAN IS LESS LIKELY TO BE ZORRO THAN DON DIEGO!

WELL, ACTUALLY, I'M RATHER FLATTERED, BUT SURELY, YOU CAN'T BE SERIOUS...

Panel 6: SEÑOR COMANDANTE! I RODE HERE AS FAST AS I COULD! HE IS ALMOST HERE! A MATTER OF HALF AN HOUR, AT LEAST!

WHAT? WHO IS HERE, STUPIDO?

THE VICEROY, DON ESTEBAN SALAZAR, HIMSELF, COMING TOWARD THE PUEBLO! / **THE VICEROY? BUT WHY IS HE COMING HERE WITHOUT WARNING?**	**H-M-M! PERHAPS MY POLITICAL ENEMIES HAVE BEEN SPREADING LIES ABOUT ME... SAYING I HAVE AN INCOMPETENT ADMINISTRATION! HA! BUT I WILL FOOL THEM!** / **WHAT ARE YOU GOING TO DO, MI CAPITAN?**
SERGEANT, WE WILL HAVE A JOYOUS RECEPTION FOR THE VICEROY! EVERYONE IN LOS ANGELES WILL BE HAPPY! OUR JAIL WILL BE EMPTY! / **BUT... BUT THE JAIL IS PACKED... AND PEOPLE ARE NOT HAPPY!**	**EMPTY THE JAIL, YOU IDIOT! TAKE THEM TO THE TAVERN FOR FREE REFRESHMENTS! THEY WILL BE HAPPY BY THE TIME THE VICEROY ARRIVES! AND I WANT THEM TO CHEER! IS THAT CLEAR?** / **YES, MI CAPITAN! I AM ON MY WAY!**
AND WHAT CAN I DO TO HELP YOUR REPUTATION, CAPITAN? / **HA! YOU, SEÑOR ZORRO, REMAIN HERE AS MY POLITICAL PRISONER! THE VICEROY WILL BE PLEASED TO SEE I HAVE FINALLY CAPTURED SUCH A BANDIT!**	*PRESENTLY, DOWN AT THE CELL BLOCK...* **COME ON OUT! YOU ARE ALL FREE!** / **WHAT? WHAT KIND OF TRICK IS THIS?**

THEY'LL SHOOT US IN THE BACK AND THEN SAY WE WERE TRYING TO ESCAPE!
AMIGOS! THIS IS A FIESTA! THE VICEROY IS COMING TO SEE US! OUR GENEROUS COMANDANTE IS GIVING FREE REFRESHMENTS TO ALL OF YOU!
HOLA! WHY DID YOU NOT SAY SO BEFORE? WE WILL GO!
A FIESTA! FREE REFRESHMENTS!
AMIGOS! WAIT FOR ME! WE WILL GO TO THE TAVERN!
TO THE TAVERN! TO THE TAVERN!
MEANWHILE, MONASTARIO'S LANCERS ARE ROUNDING UP THE CIVILIAN POPULATION...
WH-WHAT IS IT? WE HAVE DONE NOTHING!
YOU ARE TO CHEER FOR THE VICEROY! OUTSIDE, QUICKLY, WITH THE WHOLE FAMILY!
HURRY! THIS IS A HOLIDAY! ENJOY YOURSELVES! AND CHEER LOUD FOR THE VICEROY! HE WILL BE HERE ANY MINUTE!

Panel 1:
"YOU HAVE HAD YOUR REFRESHMENTS! NOW EVERYBODY OUTSIDE! THE BUGLE HAS SOUNDED! THE VICEROY IS NEAR AND I MUST ATTEND THE COMANDANTE!"

"DO NOT WORRY, SERGEANT! WE WILL CHEER... VERY LOUD!"

Panel 2:
"UH...WHAT? OH, IT'S YOU...! WELL, YOU WON'T FIND YOUR MASTER! THE COMANDANTE IS KEEPING HIM HIDDEN!"

Panel 3:
"BUT THERE'S NO WAY TO EXPLAIN THAT TO A MAN WHO'S DEAF AND DUMB! AND NOW I MUST HURRY!"

Panel 4:
SOON, AS THE CARRIAGE OF THE VICEROY COMES INTO VIEW...

"ALL RIGHT NOW, WHEN THE VICEROY'S CARRIAGE GETS A LITTLE CLOSER...EVERYBODY CHEER!"

Panel 5:
"HURRAH!" "VIVE EL VICEROY!" "VIVA! VIVA!"

Panel 6:
"GOOD WORK, SERGEANT! VERY WELL DONE! VERY SPONTANEOUS!"

"THANK YOU, MI CAPITAN!"

88

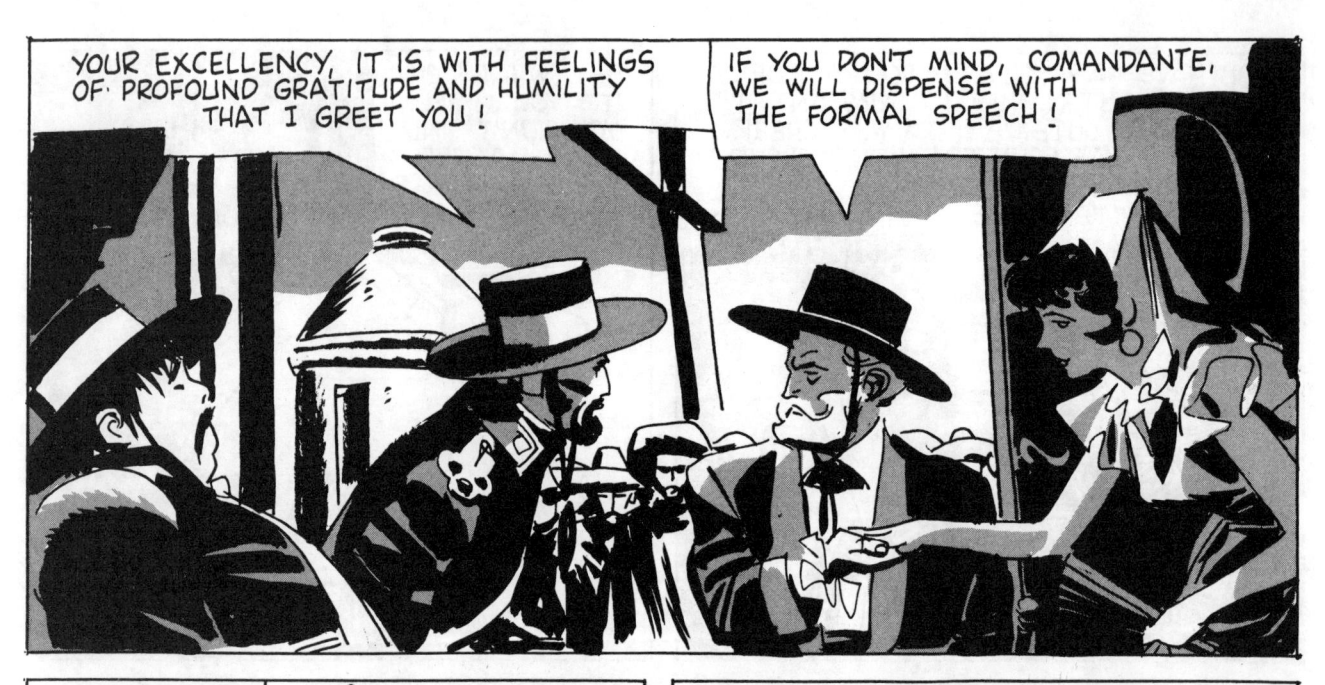

BUT WHAT OF THIS OUTLAW CALLED ZORRO THE FOX? IS HE AS FALSE AS THE OTHER CHARGES?	NO, YOUR EXCELLENCY! ZORRO IS AS CLEVER AS THE FOX! BUT I WILL HAVE SOMETHING MORE TO SAY ON THAT SUBJECT LATER!

FATHER, CAPITAN MONASTARIO HAS OBVIOUSLY PLANNED A SURPRISE FOR US!

YOU WILL SEE! BUT PERHAPS NOW YOU WOULD LIKE TO MAKE A FURTHER INSPECTION!

Soon, in Monastario's quarters...

THIS IS LICENCIADO PINA, MY PRIME MINISTER!

YOUR SERVANT, EXCELLENCY!

AND NOW, ABOUT THIS MAN ZORRO! AS YOU KNOW, HE HAS BEEN A CONSTANT SOURCE OF TERROR TO THE ENTIRE PUEBLO! HE STRIKES AT NIGHT, WHILE THE INNOCENT ARE ASLEEP! WE HAVE BEEN POWERLESS AGAINST HIM!

BUT I NOW HAVE THE HONOR TO ANNOUNCE THAT, AT THIS MOMENT, ZORRO IS MY PRISONER!... SERGEANT, BRING HIM IN AT ONCE!

HERE HE IS, MI CAPITAN! WE HAVE GUARDED HIM WELL!

THIS MAN IS A TURNCOAT OF THE WORSE SORT! A MAN WHO HELD A RESPECTED POSITION IN THIS COMMUNITY! BUT WHO...?	A YOUNG NOBLEMAN, YOUR EXCELLENCY, BY THE NAME OF...! DON DIEGO DE LA VEGA!
YOU... YOU KNOW THIS MAN? WHY, OF COURSE! DIEGO AND MY SON WENT TO THE SAME UNIVERSITY IN SPAIN!	IT IS A PLEASANT SURPRISE TO SEE YOU AND YOUR DAUGHTER AGAIN, EXCELLENCY! BUT WHAT OF THIS CHARGE, DIEGO? THE DE LA VEGAS ARE THE WEALTHIEST LAND OWNERS IN CALIFORNIA! YOU HAVE NO REASON TO TURN OUTLAW... TO ROB PEOPLE!
IF TURNING OUTLAW MEANT TO FIGHT AGAINST THE COMANDANTE'S TYRANNY, THERE IS EXCELLENT REASON! ZORRO HAS MY COMPLETE SYMPATHY, BUT UNFORTUNATELY I DO NOT HAVE HIS ACCOMPLISHMENTS!	HE LIES! PINA AND GARCIA HAVE SEEN ZORRO CLOSELY MANY TIMES! THEY COULD EASILY IDENTIFY HIM! ER...YES, MY CAPITAN! IT IS... INDEED ZORRO!

ER... DON ESTEBAN, IF YOU WOULD SEND THE COMANDANTE OUT TO COOL HIS BEFUDDLED HEAD A MOMENT, I WOULD HAVE A WORD WITH YOU!	WHATEVER THE PRISONER HAS TO SAY CAN BE SAID IN MY PRESENCE!

IT SEEMS A REASONABLE REQUEST, COMANDANTE! I WILL BE RESPONSIBLE FOR HIM!

WELL, OF COURSE... IF YOUR EXCELLENCY INSISTS... COME WITH ME, GARCIA!

AFTER MONASTARIO AND GARCIA HAVE WAITED IN THE HALL A FEW MINUTES...

THE VICEROY ASKS THAT YOU ENTER NOW, CAPITAN!

I WONDER WHAT LIES DE LA VEGA HAS TOLD THE VICEROY?

CAPITAN MONASTARIO, DIEGO HAS TOLD ME HOW YOU, YOURSELF, PROVIDED HIM WITH THIS ZORRO DISGUISE!

THAT IS SO! IT IS IDENTICAL TO THE COSTUME ZORRO ALWAYS WEARS!

I ASK YOU TO LOOK MORE CAREFULLY AT THIS DISGUISE! COULD NOT ANY MAN WEARING THIS BE MISTAKEN FOR ZORRO?

NO, YOUR EXCELLENCY! ANOTHER MAN COULD NOT POSSIBLY BE OF THE SAME HEIGHT, THE SAME BUILD, AND EVEN WEAR A MOUSTACHE SUCH AS THIS!

WELL, ONE COULD NOT ASK FOR A MORE POSITIVE IDENTIFICATION THAN THAT!

WH-WHAT?

"THEN... THEN WHO IS THIS?" "ONE OF YOUR OWN LANCERS, CAPITAN! HE ACTED ON MY ORDERS, SO NO HARM IS TO COME TO HIM!"	"ANOTHER OF ZORRO'S TRICKS! WELL, THERE'S ONE WAY TO PROVE HIS GUILT!"
"WE SHALL LET HIS EXCELLENCY SEE HOW YOU HANDLE THE BLADE! FIGHT WELL, ZORRO, BECAUSE I AM GOING TO KILL YOU!" "FATHER! YOU MUST STOP THEM!"	"I SHALL FORCE YOU TO REVEAL YOURSELF!" "REVEAL MYSELF AS A POOR SWORDSMAN? BUT YOU KNOW THAT ALREADY, CAPITAN!" CLANG
"CAPITAN! THAT IS ENOUGH! STOP!" CLANG SWISH	"NOW, ADMIT IT, DE LA VEGA! ADMIT THAT YOU ARE ZORRO!"

SUDDENLY... CRASH

IT IS ZORRO! THE **REAL** ZORRO! BUT...BUT HOW CAN IT BE?

"ZORRO" RIDES A SAFE DISTANCE AWAY AND WITH A GRIN HE UNMASKS...

BACK IN THE CUARTEL... H-M-M! THERE IS A NOTE ATTACHED TO THE ROCK!... "SORRY TO HAVE MISSED MEETING THE VICEROY!" AND IT IS SIGNED "ZORRO"!

I...I CAN'T UNDERSTAND IT!

WELL, I MUST ADMIT, YOU PUT ON A VERY CONVINCING SHOW, CAPITAN!

WHAT? A **SHOW**?

YES! YOU SEE, I ALREADY HAD MUCH EVIDENCE AGAINST YOU, AND YOUR PARTNER, PINA!... BUT IT WAS YOUR FOOLISH HANDLING OF THIS ZORRO INCIDENT THAT CONVINCED ME THAT YOU ARE AN INCOMPETENT TYRANT!

BUT... BUT YOUR EXCELLENCY...!

ENOUGH! LANCERS! PLACE MONASTARIO AND PINA UNDER ARREST!

TAKE THEM AWAY!

SERGEANT GARCIA, YOU WILL TAKE OVER COMMAND OF THIS GARRISON UNTIL A NEW OFFICER IS APPOINTED!

T-TAKE OVER COMMAND...?

YES, SIR, YOUR EXCELLENCY! RIGHT AWAY, SIR!

AND NOW WE MUST TAKE OUR LEAVE, DIEGO! I TRUST GARCIA WILL MAKE A GOOD COMANDANTE FOR A TIME!

I'M CERTAIN HE WILL, SIR! AND CONGRATULATIONS ON YOUR GOOD TASTE! YOU CERTAINLY SELECTED THE *BIGGEST* MAN FOR THE JOB!

WALT DISNEY'S Zorro

A Bad Day for Bernardo

ONE DAY IN THE PUEBLO, AS BERNARDO, DON DIEGO'S FAITHFUL MUTE SERVANT, HEADS FOR THE PLAZA TO DO SOME SHOPPING...

"LOOK OUT, PEON!"

"AIIIEEE! THAT WAS A CLOSE CALL!"

LATER, AT DON DIEGO'S HACIENDA, BERNARDO, USING HIS HANDS, DESCRIBE'S HIS NARROW ESCAPE...

"JUST MISSED YOU! LUCKY FOR BOTH OF US IT DID, BERNARDO! I DON'T KNOW WHAT I WOULD DO WITHOUT YOU!"

WHOOSHHHHH

SUDDENLY...

"DON DIEGO! A TERRIBLE THING HAS HAPPENED! MY DAUGHTER, MARIA, HAS DISAPPEARED!"

"WHEN?"

"JUST A SHORT TIME AGO! SHE WENT FOR A WALK IN THE PLAZA! BUT NOW SHE IS NOWHERE IN THE PUEBLO!"

"NOTIFY THE COMANDANTE! HE WILL HAVE THE LANCERS SEARCH FOR HER! MEANWHILE, I WILL DO WHAT I CAN!"

Panel 1:
GRACIAS, AMIGO!
SÍ!... WHAT IS THAT, BERNARDO?

Panel 2:
YOU SAY THERE WAS A BEAUTIFUL LADY IN THE CARRIAGE THAT ALMOST RAN YOU DOWN? IT WAS HEADED TOWARD SAN FERNANDO?

Panel 3:
MOMENTS LATER, IN THE SECRET ROOM...
IT LOOKS LIKE OUR FRIEND, SEÑOR ZORRO, MUST GO INTO ACTION! DON RAMON'S DAUGHTER MIGHT NEVER BE FOUND IF WE WAIT FOR THE LANCERS TO MOVE!

Panel 4:
RIDE HARD, BERNARDO! EVEN NOW THE SEÑORITA'S LIFE MAY BE IN GRAVE DANGER!

Panel 5:
MEANWHILE, IN SAN FERNANDO...
HURRY! HURRY!
PLEASE... MY ARM!

Panel 6:
STILL SEVERAL MILES AWAY, ZORRO AND BERNARDO RIDE HARD...
FASTER, TORNADO! FASTER!

BERNARDO'S HORSE HITS A CHUCK HOLE AND STUMBLES...
BERNARDO!
WHOOOOOSHH
WHAP!!
YOU SEEM BOUND AND DETERMINED TO INJURE YOURSELF TODAY, MY FRIEND!
I THINK MAYBE I SHOULD HAVE STAYED IN BED!
COME, WE MUST HURRY! I WAS IN HOPE WE COULD OVERTAKE THE CARRIAGE BEFORE THEY ARRIVED IN SAN FERNANDO!
JUST OUTSIDE SAN FERNANDO...
SOLDIERS! I WILL NOT BE ABLE TO GET INTO THE PUEBLO UNSEEN! WE MUST THINK OF A DIVERSION, BERNARDO!

Panel 1: BERNARDO HAS AN IDEA...WITH HIS HANDS, HE TELLS IT TO ZORRO...
"SÍ! THIS IS A FINE PLAN! PUT IT INTO ACTION AT ONCE!"

Panel 2: MOMENTS LATER, AT THE PUEBLO GATES...
"WHAT IS IT YOU'RE TRYING TO TELL US?"
"THE POOR MAN CANNOT SPEAK! BUT I THINK HE IS TRYING TO TELL US SOMETHING ABOUT A HORSEMAN!"

Panel 3: "Z! THE SIGN OF ZORRO! HE MUST HAVE SEEN HIM IN THE HILLS!"
"WE MUST RIDE OUT AT ONCE TO CAPTURE HIM!"

Panel 4: "BERNARDO'S PLAN WORKED PERFECTLY!"
"NOW I CAN GET INTO THE PUEBLO!"

Panel 5: "SO FAR, SO GOOD! NOW TO LOCATE THE SEÑORITA!"
ZZZZZZ

Panel 6: ZORRO SPOTS THE DUSTY CARRIAGE...
"THE HORSES OF THIS CARRIAGE LOOK AS IF THEY'VE TRAVELED FAR! WE WILL SEE WHAT THE DRIVER KNOWS!"

THIS IS ZORRO, MY FRIEND! TELL ME QUICKLY! WHERE IS SEÑORITA MORENO?
ZORRO! I...UH—
THEY...THEY WENT INTO THAT BUILDING! THAT IS ALL I KNOW!
THAT IS ENOUGH! DO NOT MOVE FROM THIS SPOT FOR TEN MINUTES OR YOU WILL FEEL THE STING OF MY BLADE!
ZORRO HEADS TOWARD THE BUILDING...
AH! I CAN EASILY CLIMB UP THOSE VINES AND ENTER BY THE BALCONY!
MEANWHILE, IN THE HILLS, BERNARDO LEADS THE LANCERS ON A MERRY CHASE...
I WONDER HOW MUCH LONGER I CAN KEEP THEM LOOKING FOR SEÑOR ZORRO...
WHAT IS THIS? WE'VE RIDDEN FAR AND HAVE SEEN NO SIGN OF ZORRO!
SÍ! IS THIS SOME KIND OF A JOKE?
SPEAK UP!
BABOSO! REMEMBER... HE CANNOT SPEAK!
AND AT THIS MOMENT I AM HAPPY THAT I CANNOT, OR I WOULD SURELY CALL THEM FOOLS!

WE'VE HAD ENOUGH OF THIS WILD-GOOSE CHASE! WE WILL RETURN TO THE PUEBLO! / AI! I MUST RIDE HARD BY THE SHORT CUT TO WARN ZORRO!	BERNARDO RIDES HARD, AND WHEN HE REACHES THE PUEBLO... WHERE CAN HE BE? I MUST...? / PSSST! BERNARDO!
DO NOT BE CONCERNED, BERNARDO! I'VE FOUND THE **SEÑORA**! / **SEÑORA**? I THOUGHT SHE WAS A SEÑORITA!	YOU SEE, JOSÉ AND MARIA SIMPLY RAN AWAY TO BE MARRIED! THEY'RE HEADING BACK TO LOS ANGELES IN A FEW MINUTES TO BREAK THE NEWS TO HER FATHER, DON RAMON!
IT CERTAINLY WAS A BAD DAY FOR YOU, BERNARDO! YOU WEREN'T EVEN HERE TO KISS THE BRIDE!	**THE END**

WALT DISNEY'S the little Zorro

One day as Don Diego and Bernardo are returning from the pueblo...

"Eh, Bernardo... it seems the little one has trouble!"

"Sob... sob..."

"What is the matter? Are you lost, little one?"

"No... not exactly, señor! It is just that I am unhappy! I have come all the way from Santa Barbara... but I cannot find the man I seek!... ZORRO!"

"Zorro! But why do you seek such a man?"

"To join with him, señor! He fights for the rights of the people! I wish to do the same! I wish for people to know the name of MANUELO!"

"Come along to my hacienda, Manuelo! After a nice hot meal, we can talk more of your wishes!"

"Sí, señor! Gracias!"

Later, at Don Diego's hacienda...

"You were hungry, Manuelo! How long has it been since your last meal?"

"I think two days, señor... and then it was just berries!"

Panel 1:
"THAT IS VERY BAD! AND IT SEEMS DANGEROUS FOR A BOY OF YOUR AGE TO BE SO FAR AWAY FROM HOME! YOUR PARENTS WILL BE WORRIED!"

"I HAVE NO PARENTS, SEÑOR! THE RANCHER WHO CARED FOR ME WAS VERY CRUEL! THAT IS WHY I RAN AWAY!"

Panel 2:
"I WISH TO MAKE SOMETHING OF MY LIFE! WHEN I FIND ZORRO, I AM CERTAIN HE WILL BE ABLE TO HELP ME! I WILL FIGHT AT HIS SIDE AGAINST INJUSTICE AND CRUELTY!"

Panel 3:
"IT IS JUST POSSIBLE THAT YOU *MIGHT* BE ABLE TO CONTACT ZORRO! WOULD THAT PLEASE YOU?"

"OH, SÍ! VERY MUCH!"

Panel 4:
"BERNARDO WILL RIDE WITH YOU TO THE MISSION! ZORRO IS SEEN THERE OFTEN!"

"GRACIAS, SEÑOR! MUCHOS GRACIAS!"

Panel 5:
A FEW MINUTES LATER, IN THE SECRET ROOM...

"IT SEEMS THAT THIS ASSIGNMENT FOR ZORRO WILL TAKE THE UTMOST TACT! THE LITTLE ONE IS QUITE SERIOUS!"

Panel 6:
"HO, TORNADO! THIS WILL BE A SHORT TRIP, BUT AN IMPORTANT ONE!"

Page 103

Panel 1:
SOMETIME LATER...
— ZORRO! IT IS REALLY YOU!
— YES, MY LITTLE ONE! ARE YOU ON YOUR WAY TO THE MISSION?

Panel 2:
— SÍ! THAT IS TRUE! I HOPED TO FIND YOU THERE! I WANT NOTHING BUT TO BE OF SERVICE TO MY PEOPLE!
— THAT IS VERY GOOD! I WISH EVERY YOUNGSTER FELT AS YOU DO... BUT ARE YOU GOING ABOUT IT THE RIGHT WAY?

Panel 3:
— I DO NOT UNDERSTAND WHAT YOU MEAN, SEÑOR?
— I MEAN YOU MUST PREPARE YOURSELF FOR SERVICE! WHAT OF YOUR SCHOOLING? DO YOU NOT THINK THAT IS IMPORTANT?

Panel 4:
— SÍ... I SUPPOSE SO... BUT...
— THE GREATEST WEAPON AGAINST TYRANNY IS INTELLIGENCE! TO GAIN THAT, YOU MUST GO TO SCHOOL... THINK... AND HAVE THE PROPER GUIDANCE!

Panel 5:
— PADRE ONORA HAS MANY BOYS IN HIS CARE AT THE MISSION SCHOOL! THAT IS WHERE YOU BELONG UNTIL YOU ARE READY TO JOIN ME!
— BUT... BUT THAT IS SO LONG! I WISH TO HELP YOU **NOW**! I WISH TO BE A MAN!

Panel 6:
— YOU MUST NOT BE IMPATIENT, LITTLE ONE! YOU ARE A BOY FOR SO SHORT A TIME! YOU ARE A MAN THE REST OF YOUR LIFE!

SUDDENLY...
SERGEANT GARCIA! IT IS ZORRO!
SÍ, BABOSO! I HAVE EYES! THIS TIME HE WILL NOT ESCAPE!
HURRY, ZORRO! DO NOT LET THEM CAPTURE YOU!
BAM!
OH! IF ANYTHING HAPPENS TO ZORRO, IT WILL BE MY FAULT! THAT CANNOT BE! I MUST HELP HIM IN SOME WAY!
I AM SORRY, BERNARDO! BUT I MUST BORROW YOUR HORSE!
Z
FASTER, TORNADO! SERGEANT GARCIA SEEMS QUITE INTENT ON HIS WORK TODAY!
BANG BANG

BAM BAM HO! THE CAPTURE OF ZORRO WILL MEAN A PROMOTION! NO LONGER WILL I BE ONLY A SERGEANT! A CAPITAN, MAYBE!	I MUST DO SOMETHING TO HELP... BUT WHAT? ZORRO IS OUTNUMBERED!
GO ON, TORNADO! LEAD THEM A MERRY CHASE! I WILL BE AWAITING YOUR RETURN AT THE HACIENDA!	ONWARD, LANCERS! THIS TIME WE HAVE ZORRO IN OUR GRASP! / POOR SERGEANT GARCIA! HE TRIES SO HARD!
THE LITTLE ONE! HE RIDES WITHOUT THINKING! HMMM? HE WILL LEARN SOMETHING FROM HIS WILD CHASE ALSO!	WITHOUT ME TO CARRY, TORNADO WILL EASILY OUTDISTANCE THE LANCERS! I WISH I COULD SEE THE SERGEANT'S FACE WHEN HE DISCOVERS ME MISSING FROM THE SADDLE! BY THE TIME HE DOUBLES BACK, I WILL BE AT THE HACIENDA!

SOMETIME LATER, AT THE HACIENDA...

SEÑORES, I HAVE NEVER SEEN ANYTHING LIKE IT! I MET ZORRO! ONE MOMENT HE WAS THERE...AND THE NEXT, ONLY HIS HORSE! THE LANCERS TRIED TO CATCH THE GREAT STALLION, BUT IT WAS LIKE GRASPING FOR SMOKE! I DID NOT KNOW WHAT TO DO!

I BELIEVE SEÑOR ZORRO WAS RIGHT WHEN HE TOLD ME I FIRST HAD TO LEARN...THEN I WILL KNOW WHAT TO DO!

THAT SOUNDS LIKE GOOD ADVICE TO ME, MANUELO!

THEN YOU AGREE WITH ZORRO'S ADVICE, DON DIEGO? IF SO, I'LL GO TO PADRE ONORA'S MISSION SCHOOL!

YES, MANUELO! MATTER OF FACT, I COULDN'T HAVE PUT IT ANY BETTER MYSELF!

THE END

WALT DISNEY'S ZORRO

THE VISITOR

ONE EVENING, AT DON DIEGO'S HACIENDA...

IT SEEMS WE HAVE HAD A VISITOR, BERNARDO! ONE WHO DEPARTS IN A MOST STEALTHY MANNER!

HO! WHAT IS THIS? MERCIFUL HEAVENS!

A BABY!

Don Diego — Please take care of my baby. I have no one else to turn to —

CARE FOR THE LITTLE ONE, BERNARDO! I WILL TRY TO OVERTAKE OUR VISITOR!

WAIT! I WISH TO SPEAK WITH YOU!

OOOOOOHHH!
ELENA LOPEZ! ARE YOU HURT?
NO, SEÑOR! IT IS ONLY MY HEART THAT IS BROKEN! BUT I HAD TO LEAVE MY BABY WITH YOU, BELIEVE ME!
COME! WE CAN TALK AT THE HACIENDA! WE WILL FIND THE CAUSE OF YOUR TROUBLE!
A FEW MINUTES LATER...
YOU SAY YOUR HUSBAND HAS BEEN IMPRISONED?
SI! JOSÉ WAS ACCUSED OF SPEAKING OUT AGAINST THE UNJUST TAXES!
NOW, I HAVE NO MONEY TO FEED THE LITTLE ONE! I...COULD DO NOTHING ELSE!
I UNDERSTAND, ELENA ...AND WE WILL HELP YOU, BERNARDO AND I! JOSÉ IS A GOOD MAN... AND A FRIEND OF MINE!
BUT...WHAT CAN YOU DO AGAINST THE KING'S MEN?
I CAN DO NOTHING, ELENA...BUT I THINK I KNOW WHO CAN!

Panel 1
"YOU REMAIN HERE, ELENA! BERNARDO AND I WILL SEE IF WE CAN CONTACT OUR FRIEND!"

"SI, DON DIEGO!"

Panel 2
MOMENTS LATER, IN THE SECRET ROOM...

"IT SEEMS OUR FRIEND, SEÑOR ZORRO, IS VERY EASY TO LOCATE, EH, BERNARDO?"

Panel 3
"LOOK AFTER ELENA AND THE LITTLE ONE! I WILL RETURN SHORTLY!"

Panel 4
ON TORNADO, THE GREAT BLACK STALLION, ZORRO RIDES THROUGH THE NIGHT...

Panel 5
AND SOON, REACHES THE WALL OF THE CUARTEL...

"AH! NO ONE IN SIGHT!"

NOW TO LOCATE MY FRIEND, JOSÉ!
AHA! IT IS MY GOOD FORTUNE THAT SERGEANT GARCIA IS ON GUARD DUTY... DOZING AS USUAL!
I WOULD HATE TO HAVE TO HURT HIM... SO, I WILL SIMPLY DISTRACT HIM!
EH! WHAT GOES THERE? I MEAN, WHO'S THAT NOISE?
WOK
SSSSWWISHH
AS THE SERGEANT MOVES AWAY...
SHHHHH!
ZORRO! I KNEW YOU WOULD COME, SEÑOR! GRACIAS!
THANKS ARE NOT NEEDED, MY FRIEND! CALIFORNIA NEEDS BRAVE MEN LIKE YOU IF WE ARE EVER TO OVERCOME INJUSTICE!

AIEEE! IT IS ZORRO AND THE PRISONER! GUARDS! GUARDS!
BAM
YOU ARE TRAPPED, ZORRO! I WILL NOT LEAVE YOU!
DO NOT BE CONCERNED, JOSÉ! MY HORSE IS ON THE OTHER SIDE OF THE WALL! WAIT FOR ME THERE!
WE HAVE HIM THIS TIME! ONWARD, MEN!
CLANG
SORRY TO DISAPPOINT YOU AGAIN, SERGEANT!
QUICKLY, JOSÉ!
STOP THEM! STOP THEM!

OH, NO! HE DID IT AGAIN! WAIT UNTIL THE COMANDANTE HEARS THIS NEWS! CARAMBA!
BLAM
BLAM
LATER...
DON DIEGO! DID YOU HAVE ANY LUCK?
NO, ELENA! I AM AFRAID MY FRIEND COULD DO NOTHING!
THEN SUDDENLY...
JOSÉ! BUT...?
ZORRO FREED ME! HE SAID I WOULD FIND YOU AND THE LITTLE ONE HERE!
BUT HOW DID HE KNOW?
HOW DOES ZORRO KNOW ANYTHING? I DO NOT QUESTION HIS WAYS! I AM MYSTIFIED BY THE MAN...LIKE EVERYONE ELSE!
I QUITE AGREE, JOSÉ! I DO NOT UNDERSTAND THE MAN AT ALL! BUT, THEN... HE AND I ARE SO MUCH DIFFERENT!

WALT DISNEY Presents
ZORRO
in A DOUBLE FOR DIEGO
EARLY ONE MORNING, A FEW MILES OUTSIDE THE PUEBLO DE LOS ANGELES...
FASTER BABOSOS! ZORRO MUST NOT ESCAPE THIS TIME!
BLAM
BAM
HO! SERGEANT GARCIA AND HIS LANCERS SEEM IN EARNEST!
BLAM
ZINNNNG
WE MUST TAKE DRASTIC ACTION, TORNADO!
AT ZORRO'S COMMAND TORNADO JUMPS...
SPLASH!

Panel 1:
CARAMBA! HE DID IT AGAIN!
HE IS HARDER TO CATCH THAN A WHIRLWIND!

Panel 2:
Later, in the secret room of Don Diego's hacienda...
INDEED, BERNARDO... IT WAS A MERRY CHASE! I ALMOST FELT SORRY FOR THE POOR SERGEANT!

Panel 3:
That night...
EH, BERNARDO... IT SEEMS WE HAVE A VISITOR!
SERGEANT GARCIA! THIS LOOKS LIKE TROUBLE!

Panel 4:
WHAT BRINGS YOU HERE AT THIS HOUR, SERGEANT... TROUBLE AT THE CUARTEL?
NO, DON DIEGO... NOTHING OUT OF THE ORDINARY... IT IS THAT ZORRO AGAIN!

Panel 5:
ZORRO? WHAT HAS HE DONE NOW?
HE HAS ELUDED ME AGAIN! IT IS GETTING VERY EMBARRASSING! MI CAPITAN IS BEGINNING TO DOUBT MY BRAVERY!

Panel 6:
MY SYMPATHIES ARE WITH YOU, SERGEANT... BUT WHAT IS IT THAT *I* CAN DO FOR YOU?
I HAVE A PLAN TO CAPTURE ZORRO, SEÑOR... AND YOU CAN HELP ME!

Panel 1:
"HELP YOU CAPTURE ZORRO? BUT... EVERYONE KNOWS THAT I AM NOT A MAN OF ACTION, SERGEANT!"
"SI! THAT IS JUST IT! THE TALES OF YOUR TIMIDNESS ARE TOLD ALL OVER THE PUEBLO!"

Panel 2:
"NOW...WHAT DO YOU THINK WOULD HAPPEN IF YOU LET IT BE KNOWN THAT YOU KNOW WHO ZORRO REALLY IS!"
"WHY...I...UH...DON'T KNOW! WHAT WOULD HAPPEN?"

Panel 3:
"DON'T YOU SEE? ZORRO WOULD COME HERE TO TRY TO SILENCE YOU! MY MEN AND I WILL BE WAITING FOR HIM! THAT IS WHEN I WILL PERSONALLY CAPTURE THE BLACK FOX!"
"A VERY CLEVER PLAN, SERGEANT!"

Panel 4:
"THEN YOU WILL GO ALONG WITH IT?"
"SI! IT IS MY DUTY TO THE COMANDANTE!"
AIIEEE! MY MASTER HAS GONE MAD!

Panel 5:
"GRACIAS, DON DIEGO! I WILL SPREAD THE NEWS! IT WILL THEN NOT BE LONG BEFORE THE FIREWORKS START!"
"ADIOS, SERGEANT!"

Panel 6:
"DO NOT BE ALARMED, MY FRIEND! I THINK WE WILL FORMULATE A PLAN OF OUR OWN!"

BERNARDO CANNOT UNDERSTAND HOW DIEGO PLANS TO BE IN TWO PLACES AT THE SAME TIME... **YES, BERNARDO... I KNOW IT PRESENTS A PROBLEM... BUT TOGETHER, I BELIEVE WE CAN FIGURE SOMETHING OUT!**	GARCIA, KNOWING THAT WORD WILL GET TO ZORRO, TELLS MANY PEONS OF DON DIEGO'S KNOWLEDGE... **YES, INDEED! AND TONIGHT THAT GENTLEMAN IS GOING TO TELL US THE REAL IDENTITY OF ZORRO!**

THAT NIGHT, GARCIA AND HIS LANCERS WAIT CONFIDENTLY FOR ZORRO TO APPEAR...

EH, DON DIEGO IS BRAVER THAN I THOUGHT! HE AND BERNARDO SIT NEAR THE WINDOW, AS IF DARING ZORRO!

SI! I WOULD NOT SO EXPOSE MYSELF TO A MARKSMAN SUCH AS ZORRO!

THEN... **PSST! HE COMES, SERGEANT!** **I HAVE EYES, BABOSO! WE WILL WAIT UNTIL HE MOVES CLOSER!**	THEN, WITHOUT WARNING... **CRASH**

116

THERE HE GOES! **NOW! AFTER HIM! PRONTO! PRONTO!**

BLAM BAM

GET HIM! HE MUST NOT ESCAPE THIS TIME!

It seems a pity to disappoint the poor sergeant again! He seems so earnest!

The next instant, Zorro ducks into the entrance to the hidden room...

FAN OUT! SURROUND THE AREA! HE CANNOT GET FAR! A YEAR'S PAY TO THE MAN WHO BRINGS HIM DOWN!

It seems strange! One minute he is here... and the next... POOF! Oh, well... He must be nearby! He cannot escape my net!

117

WHILE MY MEN SEARCH, I MUST SEE IF MY FRIEND, DON DIEGO, WAS HURT BY THE STONE! IF SO, IT IS MY FAULT...I AM TO BLAME!	*Inside...* AI'EE!! IS IT PAINFUL, SEÑOR? / NOT REALLY, SERGEANT! THE STONE DID NOT HIT ME, BUT I WAS STARTLED AND FELL OFF THE CHAIR!
THANK HEAVEN FOR THAT! YOU WERE VERY BRAVE!... BUT THE STONE — IT HAS A MESSAGE! / YES — IT SAYS "NO ONE KNOWS ZORRO!" IT IS A WARNING, I FEAR!	NEVERTHELESS, WE WILL NOT GIVE UP THE SEARCH! ZORRO WILL BE BROUGHT TO JUSTICE! / I HAVE GREAT FAITH IN YOU, MY FRIEND! BUT, AS FOR ME, I SHALL HEED THE WARNING!
Moments after Garcia has gone... AH, BERNARDO, IT IS AMAZING HOW LITTLE EFFORT WAS REQUIRED TO DECEIVE OUR FRIEND, SERGEANT GARCIA, AND HIS MEN!	ALL IT TOOK WAS JUST THE SHADOW OF THIS CUTOUT CAST UPON THE WINDOW... AND NOW, THE POOR SERGEANT WILL SPEND A FRUITLESS NIGHT CHASING A PHANTOM!

image COMICS

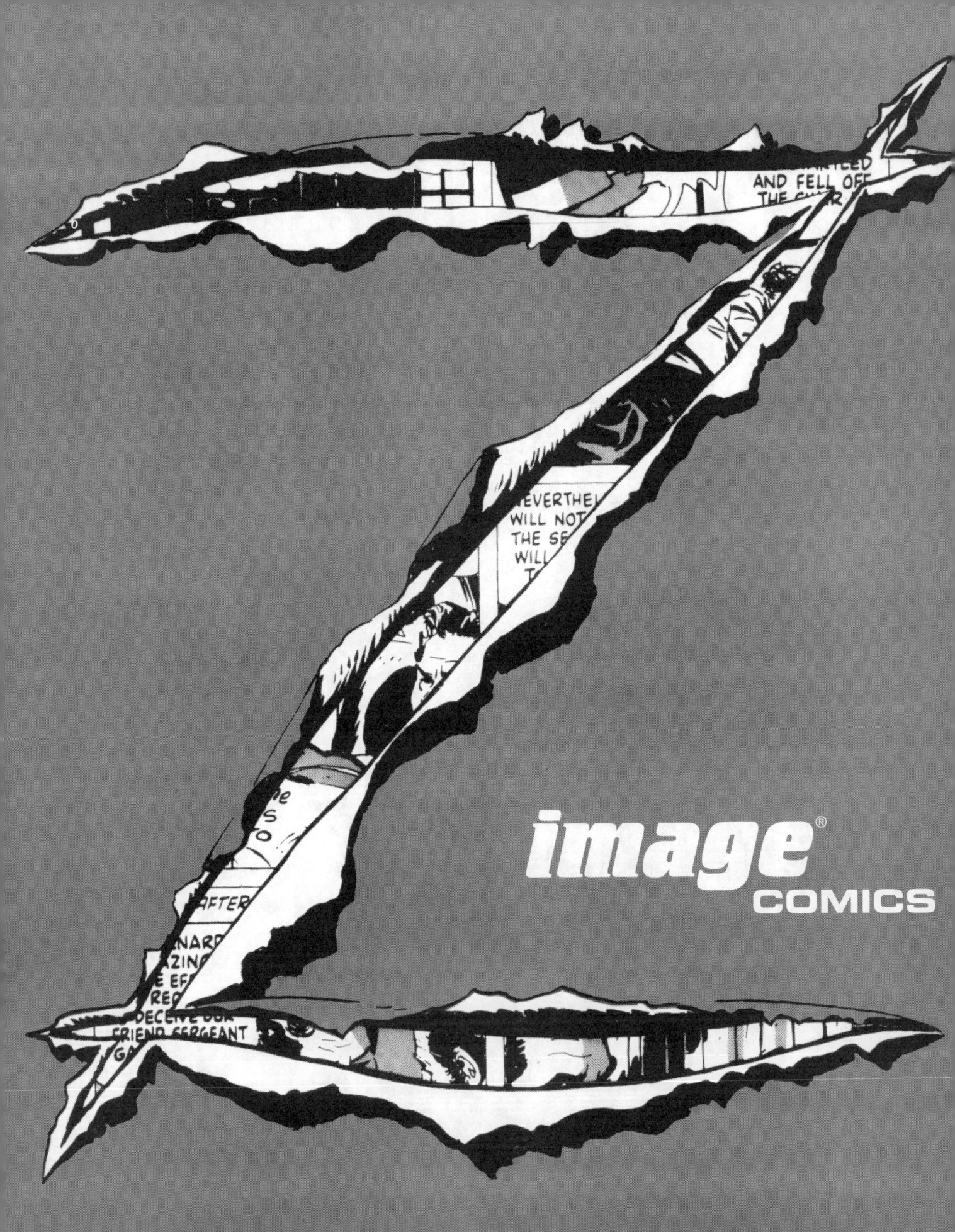